THE LEADERSHIP JOURNAL. Volume 3

Let's Connect

Compiled (and lightly edited)
by **Joy Lindsay**

with design and editing support
from **huiying b. chan** and **Cathleen Meredith**

Butterfly Dreamz ®

let's connect

This journal was created by the **youth leaders** in our Cocoon Club. There's no "right" or "wrong" way to use it. Our hope is that it'll be a powerful leadership tool for **teen girls** and their **mentors.** As you use this journal, we invite you to:

read

Read the inpsiring stories, poetry, and thoughts from the girls and young women in our Cocoon Club community.

write

Write down your own stories, poems, and thoughts by responding to the journal prompts.

color

Clear your mind by coloring the illustrations and mandalas that appear throughout the journal.

connect

Use these pages to connect with your inner self and the mentors, friends, and other loved ones in your life. Talk about the poetry, stories, and journal prompts. Share your thoughts with others and reflect on your leadership growth. If you're not already a member, join our Cocoon Club at **cocoonclub.org/join.**

write to lead
Editor's Note

Kadysia Smith, one of our Write to Lead interns writes, "Back then, she didn't carry the world, she owned it. It carried her and her imagination."

The authors of each of these pieces hold heart, courage, vulnerability, and determination. In our Saturday sessions, we gathered virtually, in a time of continued isolation and distance, to share and connect about our lives and the stories we would tell. These pieces are evidence of each author diving deep into their lives, reflecting on the stories they wanted to share with the rest of our community, and surfaced these poems, memoirs, fiction pieces. In a time of continued uncertainty, where many in our communities are looking for ways to connect, heal, and support one another, where many are also fighting for overdue societal changes, I invite you in— to the sanctuary spaces that each writer has created. May each piece move you as they have moved me. May each piece be a gentle breeze forward to continue walking proud and dreaming.

— huiying b. chan
2021-2022 Write to Lead Instructor

cocoonclub.org/**join**

contents

Take a look at the table of contents below and then turn to the **journal page** that stands out the most to you:

connecting with self

connecting with others

By Darya Mason, *Cocoon Club Member*

mental health struggles

Dear Cocoon Club,

I've really been struggling with my mental health throughout this pandemic. What are some things I can do to feel better and improve my mental health?

cocoon club responses

Dear Leader,

I'm so sorry to hear about the impact that the pandemic has had on your overall mental health. I know that it must have been extremely challenging to have to adjust your whole life to be virtual while also dealing with personal family issues. There are two things that I personally found helpful to do when I felt that my mental health was not in the best state. The first thing I suggest is journaling. Through writing down stressors in your life that are negatively affecting your mental health, it may be easier to address those issues directly. Another strategy I recommend is confiding in your loved ones. Telling someone about issues that are impacting you negatively could create space for them to give you helpful advice on ways to move forward. You are worthy of happiness and this struggle is only temporary.

Much Love,
Ruth
Community Ambassador

Dear Leader,

Some ways you can improve your mental health are by doing things like meditation and yoga. You can even listen to your favorite music, and you can communicate to others. A way I practice good mental health is by allowing myself to have time to fully understand my emotions to the best of my abilities. I have a special place where I give myself time to just feel with no prying eyes. If you can't have a special place you can go under the covers or even into the shower—somewhere where you don't have to control the way you express your emotions. I understand the hardships that come with great changes in good or bad weather. Don't be upset with the way you're feeling; instead, allow it to come and pass.

—Sanaa
Community Ambassador

Dear Leader,

I can definitely relate to you. I as well struggled a lot during the pandemic regarding my mental health. I was very depressed and didn't know how to positively cope with some of the struggles I was facing. I still struggle, but some of the things that have helped a lot in boosting my emotional and physical health is praying. As a Muslim, I like to take time to sit, reflect, and connect with God about any problems I have. I also like to read, watch movies, catch up on shows, and sleep. To feel better and improve your mental health, try doing things that you enjoy or that make you happy. This could make you feel calm and at peace. Some of our Cocoon Club members like meditating, doing yoga, spending time with friends and family, doing arts and crafts, or even journaling. There are so many ways and things you could do.

—Zaharaou
Community Ambassador

Dear Leader,

I understand times may be challenging, but you are taking the first steps to take care of yourself, acknowledging that you are struggling and need help. First, take some time to self-reflect on what is troubling you and what you could do to help improve your mental health. Think about activities that help relax you and take you away from your worries into a safe space. Some ideas are to journal, listen to your favorite music, exercise (yoga, sports, gym), or just simply sleep. For me sleep is one of the most helpful mental health practices. It allows me to recharge and gives me a space where I don't have to think about my worries or everything going on in the world. Also, the biggest thing that can help your mental health is expressing your feeling and worries to someone you trust and seeking advice from them. There are many people out there who have experienced the same thing; this pandemic has affected everyone, so don't feel like you are alone.

—Lailah
Community Ambassador

Dear Leader,

I know living in a pandemic has been difficult, and I am happy to see that you are actively working on improving your mental health. I would recommend writing. Journaling about your day, emotions, or thoughts is a great way to find calm in the storm. This is a great way to release emotions that may otherwise be stuck in your mind. This is my personal favorite mental health practice; I feel a lot better when I am able to get my feelings out by writing everything down onto something tangible. Many girls in the Cocoon Club also practice relaxation. Whether it is yoga or just simply taking a nap, relaxing your body will do wonders for your mind as well.

—Asmi
Community Ambassador

Dear Leader,

I love reading over these responses because it really shows how different we are but also our similarities at the same time. I feel there are so many things that can be a mental health practice because everyone is mentally different. For some girls a mental health practice can be as simple as sleeping or as cool as playing the ukulele. Personally, the best mental health practices for me is doing something that stops my brain from being on overload. This could be a bath or a scary movie. I think it is beautiful that we can make our own standards for how we can practice good mental health and it is good to follow recommendations too .I also think that having a daily mental health activity is outstanding. Mental health awareness has grown so much in our society but sometimes as girls and women of color, it may take a backseat to life or work. So, it is important that we can find at least one thing that helps our minds stay healthy.

—Kayla
Community Ambassador

Dear Leader,

This pandemic has been a tough time for a lot of people, and it's taken a toll on a lot of people's mental health. My advice to you is to take a deep breath, take time to relax, and find a hobby, practice, or routine that makes YOU happy. You could start doing yoga or meditating to relieve stress, boost your mood and reflect on your day. You could also do self-care: take a shower, develop a skincare routine, put on a face mask, watch movies, read a book, or snuggle under the covers. If you want good ways to relieve stress, venting to a trusted friend or adult is a good idea, or if you'd prefer to keep it to yourself, you could journal! If you think "I'm too busy to take time for myself!", change that thinking to "I deserve to take time for myself, even if it's five minutes!". Personally, my favorite mental health practices are taking walks while listening to podcasts or music, doing yoga, meditating, watching my favorite shows, and painting! They all help calm me down and allow me to rewind and just focus on one thing. I especially love meditating; it's so calming and has helped me find confidence, boost my energy, and practice gratitude. If you would like to start meditating but don't know how to, you could use the app "Simple Habit" (which I personally love) or search up starter meditations on YouTube! At the end of the day, your mental health is important, and you deserve to relax, spend time doing the things you love, and be happy.

Best wishes,
Samantha | Community Ambassador

Dear Leader,

In order for you to feel better, you need to value your personality and true characteristics, and learn how to take care of yourself altogether. Only you can take care of yourself the best because you know what's best for you. And while you're at it, appreciate who you are and what you have in life with daily affirmations. Secondly, when it comes to mental health, some Cocoon Club members find that drawing or self-reflecting (journaling) is effective. Other members also say relaxing is quite beneficial, so find what method is effective to ease your nerves and improve your mental state. In my opinion, relaxation is the best practice for me. You have the freedom to choose what you like to do and learn what will make you feel better.

—Ariana | Community Ambassador

Dear Leader,

You are doing an amazing job no matter what step you are at in your journey to growing into a wonderful, powerful, and inspirational leader! Prioritizing your mental health and well-being whenever possible during your journey will be key, but one thing is for sure: it looks different for everyone. I find that journaling each night about how my day went and what the highlights were is really helpful to me. It helps me reflect and understand myself better and the goals I need to set in the future. Once you find what works for you, dive into it with power and trust in the process. Spending time doing what you love and what makes you feel better will ultimately allow you to improve your mental health.

Warmly,
Eana | Community Ambassador

extrication

By Regan Bandy, *Write to Lead Intern*

Dear Black Girl
It's me, Mental Health.
I am always there, whether good or bad
Controlling you, day and night nonstop
I decide whether you get up and fight
Or if you just lay down and cry
I determine how miserable your days will be
This is My body and your soul merely occupies it
Playing with you like an addictive video game, hours on end
Except you can't just turn Me off
Your life is Mine to do whatever I so please
I live through you and while you may be miserable, I'm having the time of my life
Even when I give you control, I know I can take back the controller at any time
Your past claws at you as if it's trying to escape
Scratching at your insides until all that's left is shreds of what used to be you
Tearing you down, piece by piece
Little by little, scratch by scratch
Gasping for air and reaching for the surface
Just so you can stay above Me
You fight against Me every day and lose every time
Until you don't
One day you take the controller
And it's suddenly beyond my reach
The memories of me become immemorial
You break from the barriers I put you in
Like a butterfly emerging from their cocoon
Ready to soar and be all you can be

Dear Mental Health
It's me, Black Girl
You tried to tear me down and break me
Until I was nothing but a shell of what I used to be
You clawed at me endlessly
Until I finally broke free
I've taken back control of my life
You can't tear and break me down anymore
No more games, no more sad times

I've been trying to find ways to describe you
To anyone, any curious mind
I couldn't initially but now I can,
You used to be a big blue boulder
Weighted with the stresses of life
Pushing me down when I tried to arise
Before I knew it you became the tiniest pebble
One that could barely be seen by the naked eye
I picked you up and threw you in the river nearby
I watched you swim into the horizon
That's when I felt so free
And decided to take back me

journal: *What does it mean to **extricate** from something or someone? Where in your life is extrication needed?*

_____

_____

_____

_____

_____

_____

_____

_____

_____

_____

_____

_____

_____

_____

_____

_____

_____

_____

"I'M BLACK & BETTER THAN EVER."

BY LAMARTHA BOOCK

YANOVA BOOCK is an Aerospace engineer. Aerospace engineering is the primary field of engineering dealing with the design, development, testing, and production of aircraft, spacecraft, and related systems and equipment. Aerospace engineers are employed in industries in which workers design or build aircraft, missiles, systems for national defense, or spacecraft.

Yanova went through advanced training in mathematics and physics. Aerospace engineering is one of the most challenging engineering fields. In addition to designing and engineering aircraft, engineers must test the crafts for safety. This is the career Yanova has chosen for herself, and she loves it. She was born in Cameroon, Africa, raised there until she was 5, then moved to the US with her parents and big brother. When she was younger, she had always found space as this unique beautiful thing and now she gets to study it. She plans to build on this career into becoming an astronaut so her dreams and goals for herself are still very big.

At first, believe it or not, Yanova wasn't quite sure about what she wanted to pursue. She went from cashier to pilot to engineer. All it took was one visit to a space themed amusement park for her to confess she wants to study space. Though everyone has had a rough time with COVID and the 2020 year, Yanova still makes sure to prioritize her mental health. She has been on trips to places like DR, Hawaii, France, etc. She also makes sure to squeeze time in with family as much as possible. Especially her dog/best friend, "Zero." He is a beautiful black lab and basically her son.

YANOVA BOOCK

Yanova sees being Black as a blessing, she is grateful for what she has, knowing that it can be hard for other African American women to get to where she is.

Even having all these support systems you can still get knocked down in life. That has happened to Yanova; she has gone through a lot of stress and life problems but never lets that affect her work, what she does, or who she is as a person. She thanks her family and friends for being there for her no matter what. She says it is good to have a loving and available support system at all times because life can hit you with something that is unexpected. So she is succeeding at her work, proving all who doubted her wrong.

Her favorite movie is *Hidden Figures*; Yanova reminds herself everyday about the lead in the movie Mary, recognizing how much of a struggle it was to get to where she is. As a Black woman it is not easy—people waiting for you to mess up and use it as an excuse or people judging your every move and expecting nothing of you. No matter how ignorant our world can be, Yanova sees being Black as a blessing. She is grateful for what she has, knowing that it can be hard for other African American women to get to where she is. Not because they can't, but because our society won't let them.

As Yanova walks into work with her 4c hair in a bun, she stands tall and proud not letting systemic racism or some people in our society make her feel any shorter. She is proving any hater wrong and making her family proud, working on aircrafts and etc. with NASA, which has always been the dream.

journal: *Yanova believes that being Black is a blessing, despite the racism and injustices that Black women face. What part of yourself do you consider to be a blessing? Why?*

black

By Hanaa Whyte, *Write to Lead Intern*

I'm Blacker than my skin
Blacker than my momma
Blacker than my sister
Blacker is not whom I am but Black is what I am
Black as can be
Blacker than my ancestor
But you ain't Blacker than me
Black is pretty
My brown skin matches the branches on the trees
My brown eyes match the soil on the ground that brings life
My brown lips are nice and full
My brown naps and coils remind me of my grandma
My loud and proud voice reminds me of my momma
My attitude reminds me of my dad
My grandma and my momma and my dad, yeah they Black
But not Black as me
Blacker than black
Blacker than space
Blacker than you
Blacker than me

journal: *What features have you inherited from your family? Write a poem about your favorite feature and how it makes you feel.*

_____

_____

_____

_____

_____

_____

_____

_____

_____

_____

_____

_____

_____

_____

_____

_____

_____

_____

the enemy

By Kathernie Santana, *Write to Lead Intern*

My enemy, my body
How come you are part of me? But
at the same time not part of me?
My eyes are fixed on you every day
hoping that something will change
It's not worth it. Everything stays the same.
Why do I look like this? Why?

My enemy, my body
I want you to look precious
Like the stars in a clear night sky
Or maybe like those models on the ads
Who all wear an XS or an S
Those with clear glass skin
Those with no more hair than
the strands on their heads.
But no, you look DIFFERENT
Nothing I or anyone would ever ask for.

My enemy, my body
Why don't you just cooperate with my desires?
I want to be pretty, beautiful, pure
Not ugly, rusty, or dull.
I don't want to be looked at,
I don't deserve to be looked at.

Is my body at fault for me feeling this way?
I mean of course, what else would it be?
My mind? Is it my mind?
I pray every day for these answers
It's almost like looking for a needle in a haystack.
I just hate my body and its ways
Of making me feel like shit
Of making me feel worthless.

I am always thinking, searching, dreaming
for an answer. For a miracle,
that the next day I will have the body and face

I have always DREAMED of.

But is my body at fault?
Maybe I blame it
for no serious reason.
At least I am alive,
At least I am ALIVE!

These unrealistic
Standards are what is keeping me down.
It's not my body
It's not my brain
It's these unrealistic
Standards

journal: *Do you have an **enemy** that makes it difficult for you to love your body? If so, who or what is it? What actions could you take to overcome your enemy and love your body?*

_____

_____

_____

_____

_____

_____

_____

_____

_____

_____

_____

_____

_____

_____

_____

_____

_____

_____

_____

_____

practicing self-care

Dear Cocoon Club,

Everyone keeps talking about "self-care" but like, I have absolutely NO TIME to do anything other than school and work. What is "self-care" and how can I make time for it?

cocoon club responses

Dear Leader,

Self-care means taking care of your body, mind, and spirit. In other words, taking care of the physical and mental aspects of your body. A lot of the time, we tend to think that self-care only means caring for our body, but it's much deeper than that. We tend to separate the two between either taking care of the mind or the body instead of doing both. In order to take care of our body, we need to take care of our mind. Your mental health is just as important as your body. You can make time for self-care by taking breaks, managing your time, or having a specific day where you dedicate time just for yourself. Some of the ways I have self-care is by doing things that make me happy and in good spirits. I love watching movies and catching up on shows, as well as reading books. Every Friday I dedicate time to myself. I don't do any homework, I make sure I don't have any meetings scheduled on this day, and just focus on myself. In terms of self-care, everyone has their own way taking care of themselves. It's all about what you enjoy and what keeps you going in life.

Zaharaou
Community Ambassador

Dear Leader,

Self-care is what you make it. Whether you're listening to music on your way to school or going for a walk after work, it's all about making you feel good. Scheduling self-care into a busy life is hard; I get it. When there are fewer responsibilities on my plate, I schedule a day to indulge in myself mentally and physically. My favorite activities are riding my bike, shopping, journaling, dancing, and eating out. If your schedule won't allow a whole day to yourself, arrange your responsibilities in order of priority and cancel or reschedule a task of lower importance. Whether you take a day or even 30 minutes to do what makes you happy, I promise you'll feel better afterwards.

Natalie
Community Ambassador

Dear Leader,

I am really excited that you're reaching out to try and set out some time for yourself! Now to explain self-care, I would say it is having a set-aside time to do things that you personally enjoy—to have a "getaway" from your personal world of issues. I would suggest that you take time towards the beginning of the week and write out everything you have to do and find any gaps that you have throughout the week. Then, I would use those gap times to relax in whatever way you can. Some examples would be to plan a spa day to the extent that you can, based on your time and finances. You could also try just lounging around and watching a TV show. Self-care is not always what you see on social media; it's whatever you can do for yourself with your circumstances and your time. Try to find at least 20 minutes a day to yourself!

Anya
Community Ambassador

Dear Leader,

People make time even when they feel like they don't have enough of it. Whether it's just 15-20 minutes or a whole da, there are many ways to have self-care. It can be taking time to do normal activities like eating or washing your hair, but it can also be things you set aside for yourself like journaling or watching Netflix. You get to decide how you want to spend your time to de-stress and take care of yourself. Just remember, self-care isn't just physical; it's also mental. Be sure to take time for yourself, leader!

—Racquel
Community Ambassador

Dear Leader,

Self-care doesn't have to take up a bunch of time. Self-care can be short and can be found throughout the day. Listening to music while doing work, doodling, and getting ready can all be counted as self-care. Balancing school and work is hard, but finding time to do what you love during those breaks or while doing work can be the self-care that you need. Being in my junior year of high school, I have found it difficult to have time to sit down and take care of myself. As I navigate through, I have found little breaks in my life as a way to reflect. A few examples of this would be me listening to music on the way to school, reflecting on my day as I walk through the hallways, and treating myself by doing my nails at the end of the week.

—Rachel
Community Ambassador

Dear Leader,

Self-care to me is doing what you need to do to maintain you overall health and happiness. I think this should involve physical, mental, emotional, and spiritual practices. When I read over the responses from the girls in our Cocoon Club, self-care seemed to always revolve around those practices, no matter who it was. One of the biggest things that stood out to me was that for some girls, "putting yourself first" was there form of self-care. I think this is so important, and we should be able to do this more often without feeling guilty or selfish. If we don't make time for ourselves then it's going to get harder to make time for others. So, it is okay to say no sometimes and take time for yourself to do what helps you. It's okay to take care of you first. Many girls mentioned doing self-care when they're stressed. Even if it is just five minutes a day, I feel you should make self-care something you do regularly, so you are not building up to the point of being stressed.

—Kayla
Community Ambassador

When my heart breaks my world feels shattered, darkness from every corner seems to consume me. The thought of healing, getting better, and moving on is too far to grasp.

For a few days, I sink into my dark and lonely depression.
Not wanting to hear what others think or thought about the situation, trying to make me feel better. Because misery loves company, so why not share the sorrow and cry with others instead.

When I slowly snap out of the haze, pulling myself back together, realizing that there is so much potential that I am wasting while burying myself deeper in my own sorrows.

I turn around to pick myself up, dust myself off, and find myself once again.

There will be many heartbreaks, sad moments, and tribulations in life, but you have to be your own savior. Depending on yourself to make you feel better will only make you stronger.

Healing yourself must be your first priority before you can heal anything else. Because in the end, you can't fix something with broken materials; you can only make it worse.

By Adeliz Castillo, *Cocoon Club Member*

sunflower

By Galiba Anjum, *Write to Lead Intern*

The wind whispered my name as I walked through the vast field of flowers that were nowhere near-endless or golden as I chose to believe they were. The tall golden spheres offered a sense of security in burning shades of yellow and dark orange, as all four seasons splashed into one another; my choice of clothing seemed rational at this moment with different patches of colorful material that splash together like a mosaic.

I glided through the field, my golden cardigan flowing around me like a cape, as I slowly made my way higher and higher into the sky. I paused to take a deep breath and look around me. I watched nature come alive and untucked my lilac t-shirt from the confines of my jeans; I have no obligations here, I felt like a balloon that could fly away from my mind. I felt free, I felt strong, and I remembered how to find satisfaction in solitude and strength amidst a period of hardship. An eternity of memorable everyday moments had met up under gloriously ordinary circumstances; as I ran through the abyss of flowers, I thought about how my life looks through a foreign point of view— I hoped it looked like I had been painted into Sunflowers by Van Gogh himself. The sunflowers turned their faces to the sun and spelled my name, as if they had trusted their power and beauty to me.

The warmth of the sun and the flowers masked the blue sky in a gold hue. I crouched down to a smaller sunflower on the side of the road. In some ways it reminded me of myself, in a world of flowers that reached towards the sky. I sometimes felt small and stuck. Instead of landing my roots firmly in the soil, I had barely made it past the rough cement road. Despite its height and the dangers of someone stepping over it, the sunflower stood tall. I sighed as the sky above me darkened and the whispers of the winds turned into yells. For the slightest second, it seemed as if the sunflower sighed along with me; it was like it knew what was to come and the obstacles it would have to overcome. I stood up as my knees bent beneath me and I started walking away, throwing short glances over my shoulders every few seconds.

As I walked past the field I glanced back to the sea of sunflowers, my eyes gazed across the rolling clouds to where my sunflower stood. I turned to the wooden lodge house positioned perfectly outside the clean circular fence that kept the sunflowers safe and away from the rocky road. Sparing a few dollars dedicated to my hastily planned getaway trip, I bought a hand-painted charm of a sunflower. Although the piece could've been based on any of the thousands of sunflowers out there, I liked to think of it as that small, but strong sunflower I had seen earlier. I wished I could've plucked the flower from the ground and brought it back home, so it would be safe in my shirt pocket, shielded from the slashing rain and the howling winds. However, the courageousness the flower projected made me realize that it would be just fine.

I stand in front of my newly finished painting wearing the scent of early spring. I spin the remnants of my spontaneous sunflower trip years ago. The charm is the only thing that relates to my sunflower, yet I'm sure if I were to visit it today, tomorrow, or another few years later, it would still be standing tall. My heart has gained the same courage I discovered within the sunflower and found its passion, just like a sunflower that finds its way to the sun.

Illustration design by Galiba Anjum

journal: *If you were a flower, what type of flower would you be? How does your selected flower represent your true self?*

THE STORY OF A MODEL ON THE RISE

BY AMARI RUFFIN-AUGUSTIN

Dominique was a basketball sensation at a young age, on the rise to become something great, and she was separated from her parents when she was younger. Dominique has known since she was a child that she would grow up to be someone more. Despite the fact that she was a black girl living in Texas who traveled from state to state to see her parents and family, she made an effort to defy the current norm. Dominique persuaded her ambitions in basketball as she grew older and extended it to her modeling profession. As a rising model, she is strutting the runway and erasing all divides in the community.

Dominique is a Sorority Queen that fights for whatever causes she believes in. She makes an effort to improve her community and expose her genuine narrative while living in Texas and still traveling back and forth with her parents. Dominique's father, Rodney, works at the port of Newark and provides for his family, but she still wants more and to do more to aid her community and family. As a woman of color, she values this because she wants to strive for something bigger and better than herself. Dominique talks about leadership in her community and her sorority, which taught her strength. She is the epitome of a lady who can overcome any obstacle in her path.

She struggles for self-determination and whatever else she needs to accomplish in the long run. People often inquire about how a basketball player became a model, and she responds that it needed leadership, strength, and the ability to overcome all of her career hurdles, as well as many others. Dominique has recently begun to develop her own brand in order to demonstrate that she is capable of overcoming any obstacle. With just starting this and pushing for additional things in her community, her business has grown significantly. Dominique aspires to be the greatest and nothing less. A woman who doesn't wear her crown, she argues, is just another lady who doesn't believe in upending the existing status quo. That is why she has made it her duty to overcome any barriers that stand in her way.

DOMINIQUE RUFFIN

Transforming from basketball player to model requires leadership, strength, and the ability to overcome.

journal: *When reflecting on her career journey, Dominique Ruffin says it has required leadership, strength, and the ability to overcome? Can you relate to any of these qualities? If so, how?*

finding motivation

Dear Cocoon Club,

Everything sucks right now. I don't feel motivated to go to school or to do anything at all. What should I do?

cocoon club responses

Dear Leader,

I'm sorry to hear that you have been feeling unmotivated lately. It is important to take the time to reflect on your mental health and how you are feeling at the moment. Prioritize your overall well-being over anything else! After you have taken the time to reflect on what is causing you to feel unmotivated, try to address this issue head on so it is not something that is constantly recurring. And lastly, you need to remember why it is that you are working so hard in the first place. It is extremely easy to get overwhelmed with whatever may be going on in your life; keeping your goals in mind is the key to staying strong through your storms. I also recommend reaching out to a friend or loved one who can support you when you're feeling unmotivated. You are awesome and this one moment of feeling unmotivated does not define you! Rooting for you always. 💕

Much love,
Ruth
Community Ambassador

Dear Leader,

I know exactly how you feel. Sometimes it's hard doing your regular activities because of your mental health. Trust me, I can totally relate. You might feel like you should give up and stop trying, but I'm here to tell you: don't quit. Keep going. Cry it out and talk it out today, but tomorrow I want you to take each task one by one and give it your absolute best. You might feel like crap babe, but you'll thank yourself in the long run. I know we've all heard, "Sometimes you got to do things you don't want to do." It's true. Babe, motivation is not always available; it's discipline that helps you in the long run. Think about your goals and whom you're accomplishing these goals for. Whether it be for your family, pet, friends, or yourself, keep your end goal in mind and envision yourself accomplishing that goal. I promise you, not only will you complete that goal, you'll feel awesome you did it despite your lack of motivation.

Tyliah
Community Ambassador

Dear Leader,

I know it's hard to feel motivated sometimes and that life may seem out of your control. One thing that has helped me stay motivated was thinking of the future. When things get out of hand or just hard, thinking about the future can help remind you of the dreams you have and the steps needed to reach them. Getting motivation doesn't always have to be focusing on your future; it can be talking to friends and family as they support you through your journey. Sometimes self-motivating by writing affirmations and self-reflecting, even if things feel tedious, can lead you to heal and move forward in life with positivity.

Rachel
Community Ambassador

Dear Leader,

First thing's first, remind yourself that it's normal to feel this way. At some point in our lives, we all feel some type of way and wonder why, or what we could do to fix it. When I get into any sort of slump, I tend to stress a lot, then stress to get everything done. However, when I end up stressing about everything, it almost always leads to me not doing what I need to do to stay productive, which ultimately is not what we want. During these times, I meditate to remember the peace I have within myself and everyone/everything around me. Another way to get motivated is to just have some fun and do something you love to do. Personally, for me, that would mean baking, reading, or hanging out with friends. I know life can get really stressful, especially if you have goals and/or dreams you want to accomplish. However, bumps in the road will never be the end. If you believe in yourself and who you are, there will always be a solution.

I could tell you so many different ways to feel motivated, however, ultimately the only one who can truly figure out how to get you out of a slump and continue to strive forward and be the best version of yourself is you and only you. Of course, you will always have the support of your family and friends, but it's a process that requires time and dedication. Just go with the flow and everything will be just fine.

—Evelyn
Community Ambassador

Dear Leader,

You can gain motivation by journaling and writing out your emotions and goals. This will allow you to get whatever is on your shoulders out and let you see where you want to go moving forward. Feeling motivated is something that I have also struggled with as a senior in high school. I have gotten senioritis, which makes me not want to do what I need to get done. I feel over it or that I'll do it right before it's due. But what motivates me is planning out my future, like having a picture board or even a list in my notes or diaries. These things motivate me to strive for the things I want to achieve in my life. I think you should allow yourself to have breaks when needed but also remember to keep your priorities in check. It's not easy, so don't be upset when you fail. Instead, learn from mistakes because it's trial and error.

—Sanaa
Community Ambassador

Dear Leader,

I am so happy you decided to reach out. Having dealt with a lack of motivation myself, especially with this pandemic, I completely understand not knowing what to do to fix it. If the option is available to you, I would take some time away from school and make just a day or two dedicated to yourself. Try to at least do one or two assignments that are not too time-consuming during those days you're not physically or virtually in class—mainly finishing assignments you know that you have the energy to complete. I would also speak to your parents and your teachers/school administration. Tell them what's going on and how you have been feeling lately; see if you all can devise a plan for you to complete your schoolwork in a way that can be acceptable for everyone. Knowing your own circumstances, only you can make the final decision on what's best for you to do.

—Anya
Community Ambassador

I was lost. I was whoever they wanted me to be until I couldn't. When I was in kindergarten, if you asked me where I'm from, I'd proudly say, "Niger," because it looked a lot like "Nigeria," and I couldn't tell the difference. Nevertheless, I was excited to tell how we came when I was three and share stories of home only my mom remembered.

Then middle school came. Being dark-skinned meant you were African, and there was something terrible about that. I'm not dark-skinned, so I was in the clear. But looking around, I knew I was different. Something wasn't right. I wasn't like them. In 6th grade, I finally knew what was wrong with me. My nose was a disfigured blob in the middle of my face. My favorite part of my face, I grew to hate the most: my lips.

Classmates said, "You got DSL."

I won't tell you what that means, but I hated my reflection because of it.

I was a blank page, floating in the middle of me and who I should be.

At school, I sat through the torture of the African butt-scratcher jokes. My mind was filled with laughter, anything to distance myself from the jokes. Anything to remind me I wasn't African. To survive, when people would ask me where I'm from, I'd answer with, "Where do you think?"

To some, I was Jamaican; to others, I was mixed. To everyone, I was anyone but me, and that was all that mattered.

But it was hard. I wasn't them. I didn't get why their tales of "home" didn't sound like mine, why our dinners weren't the same, why I talked differently. So, I watched, I took notes, and I copied.

In 7th grade, I found out I'd be going to a new school. I could start over. I restocked my closet, made more observations, and learned.

It didn't work. I wasn't enough. Some saw right through me. To the few who asked, "Are you African?" I shook my head no. That word held shame and self-hate; I wanted nothing to do with it. They'd sigh in relief. I'd exhale. I was safe.
The differences became glaring, our cultures weren't the same. I'm falling at the seams, filling my mind with lies, anything to be a part of them
.
Finally, in high school, for the first time, I meet Nigerians who weren't family. My heart sank. I wasn't Nigerian enough. But I'm not African American. I'm just here floating in the in-between. However, it's a big first step.

I'd love to say there was a moment it all hit me, where imaginary light bulbs flickered brightly, and gears started to turn, but it wasn't like that.

It was a slow, painful acceptance: I could only be me. That thought first frightened me: it was a condemnation that I'd be forever trapped in this body.

Slowly, it washed into "this is me; this is who I'll always be." No excitement, no dread at the thought, just simply taking in that truth. Then my breathing slowed, the weight of the hateful words and poisonous thoughts echoing through my brain became less important. I realized I had the power.

As long as I tied my value to how I look or where I'm from, I'd never be enough. Not to anyone nor myself. I couldn't make myself more American or more Nigerian. I could only accept me. This is the only me I'd ever get, and how could I hate it when it felt like everyone else did too.

Who would show me kindness if I couldn't show it to myself? And then my eyes glowed, my lips curving into a smile, as I thought, "This is me."

A step away from years of self-hate, one towards self-discovery, walking the road to self-love; it's been tough, but if you ask me where I'm from, I'll say "Nigeria."

By Vanessa Iwuoha, *Cocoon Club Member*

the girl on the other side of the mirror

By Kadysia Smith, *Write to Lead Intern*

Blurry from scarce white smudges that cloud the vision on the other half of it; stained. Zigzag and other non-straight lines cover whatever the smudges couldn't get to. The shushing sound from the faucet snaps me back to reality. My knuckle whitening grip on the sponge in my right hand and spray bottle in my left loosens as my thoughts come from out of their abyss. *Broken and stained, huh?* Out of all of my thoughts, these are the ones that linger.

Lowering my face away from it, I place my cleaning supplies on the counter, and turn off the faucet. *There's so much more to clean. I'll come back to this.* However, in the back of my mind, I know that I'll do whatever it takes not to come back to it. My back faces the crumbling mess of glass that holds not a single good memory as I walk towards my tub. I kneel down onto the cold tiled floor, absentmindedly caressing the edge of the tub with my gloved hands. Not too long ago, I was in here singing my heart out to a song I barely know the lyrics to with a smile so bright it could put the sun to shame.

This deserves to be clean. My hands find the bottle of bleach, sprinkling generous amounts inside of it. A calm feeling wraps me in its warm embrace as my mind takes a familiar stroll through memory lane. Who knew that a tub could bring back so many nostalgic memories? Dark rusty **stains** coat over certain areas by the drain and faucet from years of too much water. Some tiles surrounding the tub walls are **cracked** or **dirty** from whoever used it previously.

Broken and stained. I shake my head, trying my best to disregard those words. *The mirror is broken and stained. It holds no good memories.* A smile tugs on my lips as my eyes notice the now faint paint stains on the inside of the tub from my younger days. My parents were repainting the rest of the house and I remember how unfair I thought it was that the bathroom was left out. Especially the tub where I always had my biggest adventures with my Barbies and other bath time toys. I took my paint brush and unskillfully painted along the inside of the tub, not doing much damage due to being caught.

Still to this day, I think a grey tub would've been a nice touch. My body shakes slightly with quiet laughter at the memory and how upset and frantic my parents were when having to remove the paint. Either that or the time I brought my dolls into the bath for a pool party. Every young girl's dream. As I use the water from the bath's faucet to rid the tub of its grime, I imagine that young girl enthusiastically preparing for her next milestone adventure with a missing tooth grin and not an ounce of the world on her shoulders.

Back then, she didn't carry the world, she owned it. It carried her and her imagination. I use the edge of the tub as leverage to help myself up off the now slightly warmer floor. Here lies the place of my childhood. Giving the edge of the tub one last caress, I wander off towards my next path of memory lane. The large bathroom wall.

My rubber covered fingertips hover over the piece of chipped lavender paint that I always pick at. I remember when we were debating on colors to paint the house with, my mother was very adamant about keeping the color lavender, for some unknown reason. But we all know that such a bright color would be hard to maintain in such a disastrous and very unsanitary area. I press down on the peeling piece of paint, trying to stick it back onto the wall. I really do need to stop destroying the image of it. Either I stop or my mom would stop me herself, and I definitely don't want that.

Skipping over to the sink to plug the drain, I pause, immediately locking eyes with the mirror once again. I can see her there. She's blurry, and I can't tell if she's scratched up or if it's the cracks on the mirror, but she's there. I can't tell the mirror's flaws apart from my own. Unsure where I begin and where the mirror stops, but I know that she feels the same way I do.

I want to reach out to her. The girl on the other side of the mirror. To tell her something. Anything would do, but where would I even start? Even now as we stare at each other, it feels like a huge miscommunication.

We're here eye to eye, or well, more like eyes to filth, but it still feels so distant. *When did you get so far away?* It takes a while, but eventually I manage to look away. For the sake of keeping the bathroom clean, I have to stay away from the mirror.

I wet the wall's washcloth with warm water then walked back to it. Luckily, there isn't much to clean. I start with what I can reach, doing side to side motions as I focus on my task. On the crease of the wall closest to the door, there's lines that were made with permanent markers. Each line is a different color and a symbol of change. I don't remember my first stages of life and I can just barely catch a glimpse of who I was when I was five to eight years old.

However, ages ten to fourteen, I do remember. At age ten, there's an orange line followed by *48 inches.* Not too far off from average height. Let's see, at age ten, I was in my Barbie phase still and I had an obsession with bobos or berets. My hair is on the kinky 4c side, so naturally I've always had to have it in protective styles. My mom would do these box twist things, but not like the popular style today. They were kind of big and slightly embarrassing.

At eleven, I had bangs and I was getting into wedges. I also had a thing for oversized sweaters, which never changed. According to the line directly above the orange one, I had only grown an inch that year. Those years were simpler. Just hanging out with friends. Especially the ones I still had from elementary school.

I had this one friend at the time, and I was always over at her house. There was no stopping me. Actually, it wasn't until recently or well, two years ago when I was sixteen, that we stopped being as close. She was the reason I got into things like music, food, even… girls, but that's not a path I want to think about. *Simple, simple, simple*. Yes! Back to when times didn't revolve around relationships or body types.

I didn't even know what a body type was until middle school. Around eleven or thirteen years old, was when I first learned the word fat. Who knew that fat and society didn't mix? Who planned on telling me? OH! I'm getting ahead of myself. I didn't learn the word **FAT** first, no. I learned the word **RACE**.

If you're Black then you have to be brown skin or dark skin, but don't make it too dark because then you'll get made fun of. Yet, if you're light skin, then you're white passing or mixed. Still to this day, I can't really wrap my head around these words. What part of my skin made my race invalid? At eleven, I was more extroverted due to elementary being such a breeze.

My friends at the time would say all kinds of things about other people and each other. Not all of them were nice. I wish all of them were nice. The first time the word **FAT** burned itself into my vocabulary, was when I had a crush on a boy whose face I can't even remember now. I remember overhearing him telling his friends that he would be with me if it weren't for the fact that I was **FAT**.

Was that really the first time I heard the word? I wreck my mind for the first time I actually heard it. My hand that is holding onto the washcloth never stops wiping down the walls even though my mind is elsewhere. I think the first time I heard the word was at home when "You got fat," was taken too lightly due to my naïveté, but it didn't get pieces together until that time with the faceless boy. **FAT** meant **BODY**.

Better yet, **FAT** meant **MY** body. That was the first step into actual adulthood. It wasn't getting my period, which wasn't even something to write home about. It was this, when I learned the difference between who I thought I was and who I am seen as. At that time, I knew that I was a **FAT** girl. However, I believe my mind over exaggerated it, but what can I do when I started to realize that most of my friends were skin and bones? It's not like I got any lighter since then either.

I grew to be more self-aware. Pushing myself out of my childish ways, I dropped all connections with my younger self. Barbies were replaced with bath bombs until baths were replaced with long showers. That was the turning point that I never noticed. Those embarrassing twists became box braids and before I knew it, I was fourteen and learning how to blend in with society.

Society wanted light skin and thankfully my mom didn't give me too much melanin. Society wanted long hair, so my braids grew long with hair extensions. Yet, there was one thing that society wanted that I couldn't give it. Society wanted skinny. Slim girls with big butts and boobs. Like a disproportionate Barbie doll. Now that I think about it, why are Black Barbie dolls always on the uglier side? Nope. Not diving into that either.

Besides my chubby stomach and arms, I did meet the rest of society's body standards. There's so much wrong with society. Unsurprisingly, fourteen is where the lines stop. Marking my height was said to be childish by my best friend at the time. Anything involving the past was childish until we were reminiscing on the way we used to be.

My best friend was my biggest influencer. We did everything together, so naturally when she dropped her childhood, I did too. She made me self-aware, even though a lot of things outside of her played a part in that too. She taught me that insecurities can be covered by new sneakers and beauty products. I was skeptical at first or better yet not interested. I didn't like the idea of wearing makeup.

New sneakers, that's a different story. I love new sneakers! ... From Payless at the time. Until I learned that they were cheap and off brand, so I had to put on Jordans. Then I learned that Jordans make friends. So if Jordans make friends then I don't have to worry about my looks. With this discovery, I acknowledged that she was right.

Curiosity killed the cat when I wanted to know what everything else would bring you. Makeup brings boys. The right clothes bring confidence. A fresh hairstyle puts everything together. I wasn't a kid anymore. When I was supposed to be a kid, I was dancing my way through society. I stopped being a kid way too early. I frown at the wall at the realization.

The wall is now spotless. All there's really left to do is clean the sink and mop the floor. I put the washcloth on its hanger that's on the wall. Mopping the floor is last, so I head over to the sink again. Cosmetics are everywhere on the counter. Eyeshadow, concealer, lip gloss, lipstick. You name it and I probably have it. I begin putting everything in its rightful spot in its decorative bins.

A glittery lip gloss catches my eyes. I pick it up, feeling a soft smile of recognition tugging at my lips. The sticker of Ariel that's on the cap is smiling at me as if she's asking me to try it on again for old times' sake. I think about it, imagining the six year old me that would come rushing into the bathroom to put on her lip gloss set. The difference between makeup then and makeup now is that makeup wasn't used for impressions back then like it is now.

Everything was tied to princesses or some kind of cartoon because that's what you knew you wanted to be and now makeup is what we use to become someone that's more comfortable with being seen. Even though most of us have no idea of what we want to be or who we are.

It's pretty funny how as a child we tend to have a lot of self-love, and as we get older, we try to fit older into society's standards. I stare at the mirror. *If this girl is me then what part of me is she?*

I find myself wetting another cloth, sudden determination races through my body. *Is she what society made or is she still holding onto the little girl that somehow always has pieces of her lingering around the bathroom as though she doesn't want to be forgotten?*

My hand hovers over the mirror, doubt and slight insecurity slipping in. I'm sure she looks no different than the last time I saw her, but something about this time just feels different. I'm not sure what I should expect. *It's only a mirror. That girl is me, right?* A quick pep talk has me finally pressing the cloth onto the glass.

Starting from the top, I can feel every crack, but to my shocking discovery it isn't as broken as I thought it was. The streaks in the mirror are small, noticeable, but only if you feel them. I take my time cleaning it, trying my best to scrub away all of its filth. Slowly, my appearance makes itself known. Braided hair that reaches my back, brown eyes that aren't too dark, so they don't look black. *She's me.*

The longer I stare at her, the more I can finally find the words I want— No, *need* to say. The clearer the words get, the more I can feel them climbing up from my throat and walking onto my tongue.

"I'm sorry."

Silence follows after my words, but she smiles. She smiles as though she's been wanting to hear these two words for so long. I know that she understands what I'm apologizing for without explanation. Her shoulders relax and her posture straightens. *Confidence.* The visible weight on her shoulders has lessened.

My eyes look around the bathroom. I gradually begin to notice that it isn't just the mirror that's broken or stained. A huge part of me knows that as I get older, I will always be broken or stained. I take off my gloves and twirl the lip gloss in between my fingers. I twist open the cap then lean forward to apply the gloss onto my lips. The lip gloss is sticky and clear, just how I remember it being. Almost stiff like (due to it being cheap) when you apply it to your lips.

For a second, I swear that I can see my younger self dressed in her Ariel costume unaware of me as she applies the same gloss onto her lips. *I will never forget about you ever again.* I swear to myself because that girl is part of who I am and it's impossible to become who I'm supposed to be without her. The same goes for the girl in the mirror. I think it's time to grow the courage to finally talk to her.

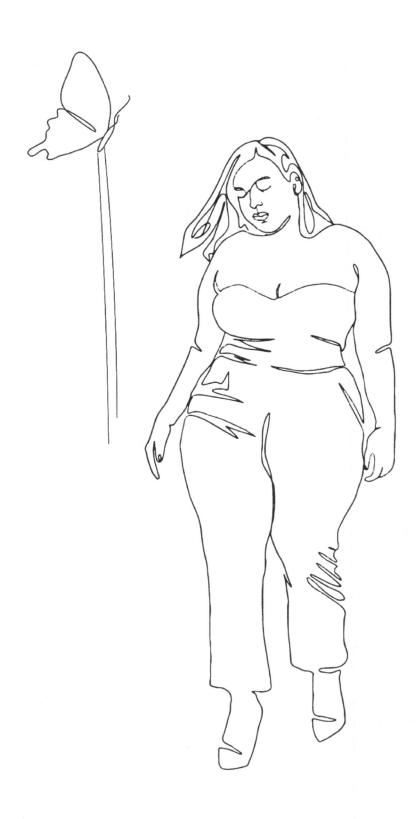

journal: *Look in a mirror for a few minutes in silence. What thoughts come to mind as you look at yourself? What do you need to say to the person staring back at you?*

CELEBRATE YOURSELF:
BEST PRACTICES FROM A BLACK FEMALE POLITICIAN

BY DANIELA PALACIOS

LaMonica McIver is the the youngest woman and Council Member to serve on the Newark Municipal Council. LaMonica McIver was born and raised in the Central Ward of Newark, NJ. Newark is the largest city in the state of New Jersey with a population of about 281,000 residents. She serves as a public educator and advocates for social justice and education. McIver continues to live in the Central Ward with her daughter.

LAMONICA MCIVER

"When working in the field of public service, it is always a resilient situation."

As a woman in politics, her work in public service always requires resilience. Councilwoman McIver emphasizes the importance of remaining confident in your opinion and not letting opposing views shift your ideas. Within the topic of housing, Councilwoman McIver strongly believes that "Newark residents deserve to have their basic needs met to live comfortably in their apartments." She describes how she holds landlords and developers in the city accountable for their actions in maintaining the quality and sanitation of their buildings.

As a Councilwoman, McIver has made strong efforts to connect with the Newark community, especially those from the Central Ward. She has built motivation in residents to really care about political activity at the local level. Among her many projects, she has helped plan the top 100 goals for the City, as well as has hosted a multitude of community meet and greets and community meetings. She advises young girls of color to "find out who your representatives are" and engage in those circles through opportunities like youth groups, nonprofits like Butterfly Dreamz, community readings, and volunteering initiatives.

During the pandemic, McIver found it important to stay encouraged, be encouraged, and stay spiritually connected. She emphasized the importance of celebrating victories, and she believes that young girls and women of color need to display this more and celebrate one another, so we can understand that we can all be victorious.

McIver describes how older women of color, she feels, don't celebrate their accomplishments enough. As one continues through adulthood, it can become a particularly difficult task to make time to focus on one's personal journey. One of the reasons this could be is because "they think they are boasting, but at the end of the day I truly think that they need to be doing it." McIver further describes how celebration can look differently depending on who you are and what you value. Celebration can range from having your ideal birthday party, prioritizing self-care, treating yourself, or practicing positive words of affirmation. Furthermore, McIver reminds girls and women of color that while we should celebrate ourselves and each other, we must also remain focused on our goals and not get too distracted with celebrating before reaching the finish line.

McIver has made a positive impact within the Newark community through every aspect of her life: educationally, professionally, and socially.

journal: *Councilwoman McIver believes that women and girls should celebrate ourselves and each other. Do you ever find it challenging to celebrate yourself or others? Why or why not?*

_____

_____

_____

_____

_____

_____

_____

_____

_____

_____

_____

_____

_____

_____

_____

_____

_____

_____

If I could tell my high school self some advice, I'd tell her it's okay to be no one.

You don't have to be the best, be your best. Do the things that make you happy. And maybe, shock others when you do extraordinary things. Because you see, my friend, when you fight the relentless fight of being the best, you kill your soul, your creativity. You render the talents of your heart as drawbacks to imagined success. Every decision is well-thought and drawn out. But, my dear friend, that is far from reality, it's your own contrived fallacy. Life is explosive, it's spontaneous, and it spits on our plans and schedules. It rains on parades and sprinkles sunshine on snowy lands. Life is alive and it screams, shouts, yells—no it begs us, pleads—that we follow its funny improvisations.

But you impose to do the opposite, you impose to design your silly plans and imagine the outcome of every day. You beg to differ; you must plan the future to own the future. And there, my friend, is where I must stop you.

You cannot own the future, not even the past nor the now. My friend, you are implying you can own time, but you can't. It is an unimaginable force of its own, it's neither alive nor dead and it flies. No, it soars, and it spins through experiences, memories, and entire galaxies. It flies and it soars with a mind of its own and you will die a sad death if you think you can ever get a hold of its incredible flight.

You open your mouth, you want to speak, shout, but there isn't much to say. In fact, there's nothing. You know I'm right; you know the way the clock flies right past you.

"So, what do I do?"

Your lips are pursed but your eyes, they tell a story of their own. They sing the sweet melody of despair. They tell the story of one who's never lived anywhere outside their own head. You've been walking amongst the living yet living in a cage you designed all on your own. You've trapped yourself and rendered yourself an outcast because you've failed to meet your own impossible expectations.

Tears slip down your cheek as I look you up and down.

"Well, what do I do?" Your voice cracks and your head swings to the ground.

"You can't tell me it was all for nothing," you say.

I sigh. Your head swings as you rain into your palms.

Breathe, I tell you. In and out. Slowly. There's no rush. We have time.
Your breaths are scattered and shaky, they're volatile, and they're close to another breakdown. I must choose my words carefully or I might be your undoing.

My friend, you have all the power. Like I said, it's all in your head. So, my dear, let go of what others have told you that you need to accomplish. Let go of your attachments to your abilities. And be.

"And be?" It's like you ignored everything else.

My friend, I say sternly, listen to every word.

You're silent, but your head slowly raises and your shoulders rise. You nod.
Dream big. Like time, soar far beyond your imagination and limitations. Quiet the noise of the outside world while still living in it. Quiet that voice in your head, tune in to your heart, to your inner child. And be.

Write your dreams and how to get them. Make a plan—yes I said "plan"—and understand that things will change. The steps may change, your dreams may change, you may change. But invest in time, rather than spend it. Dedicate every day as another step toward your dreams. Believe in the flight of time, let it carry you through your journey. And, my dear friend, don't forget to be.

By Vanessa Iwuoha, *Cocoon Club Member*

highs, lows, sheroes

Let's Connect: *Do you have any highs, lows, or sheroes this month?*

- *high = highlight from your month*
- *low = low point of your month*
- *shero = woman or girl who supported you this month*

💭 my thoughts

cocoon club ideas: *How could you **celebrate** your "highs"?*

- *Have a picnic with friends or by yourself*
- *Do something that you're passionate about (e.g. dancing)*
- *Take yourself on a dinner date*
- *Have a spa day with friends or by yourself*
- *Buy yourself your favorite flowers*
- *Buy yourself something you've been wanting for a while (e.g., new shoes, a purse, earrings, makeup, etc.)*

                —Garnisha, *ExCEL Fellow*

- *Host a Girls' Night at your house (e.g., movie marathon, dancing, makeovers, homemade pizza, etc.)*
- *Pick up an old hobby or start a new hobby (e.g., knitting, yoga, new language, photography)*
- *Redecorate your room*
- *Visit a fun, local spot (e.g., movie theater, arcade, concerts/festivals, bowling, escape room, etc.)*
- *Take a day trip (e.g., beach day, amusement park, aquarium, etc.)*

                —Jade, *ExCEL Fellow*

lead the way: *What **creative gift** could you make for your shero?*

- Homemade card, sharing words of thanks and special memories
- DIY personalized gift box with thoughtful items (e.g., scented candles, special photos, favorite flowers, baked goods, etc.)
- Self-made artwork
- Hand-knitted item (e.g., scarf, book cover, slipper boots, etc.)

—Jade

- Care package with beauty essentials ("self-care basket")
- Homemade edible arrangement with your shero's favorite fruits
- Thoughtful hand-written letter about how your shero has impacted your life
- A decorated jar with daily affirmations that your shero can pick from everyday
- A painted picture frame with a picture of you and your shero
- Homemade candles

—Garnisha

🗯 *my thoughts*

By Judea Green,
Cocoon Club Member

making new friends

Dear Cocoon Club,

My family just moved to a new city and now I'm the "new girl" at my high school. It's the middle of the year so everyone already has their friends, and I'm not sure I fit in here. I'm from a small town and this is a big city. Any advice on how I can make friends?

cocoon club responses

Dear Leader,

The most important thing to do when making friends in a new environment is to be your most authentic self. If you are true to yourself, you are bound to find the right people for you. Also, sometimes we tend to be shy in these situations; the best thing to do is push yourself out of your comfort level and be direct. I completely understand not feeling like you fit in, but remember that you belong in any space you are in. I started at a new school when I was in 6th grade and was scared of how I would make friends and adapt to a completely new environment. I pushed myself out of my comfort zone and forced myself to go up to people with no worries or expectations in mind. In fact, the person I said hi to ended up being my best friend for seven years. Don't be afraid to go up to someone, say hi, and start a conversation. They could end up being your best friend. But if you find it hard to do this, there's also many other ways to make friends. Try joining different clubs or taking part in other extracurriculars to find people with similar interests to you.

Lailah
Community Ambassador

Dear Leader,

I know it's hard to be the only new person in the middle of a school year, but you got this! When you are in a new environment looking to make new friends, we recommend that you be yourself and be open to trying out new things, joining clubs, and taking unique classes. Putting yourself out there and taking positive risks will allow you to find like-minded individuals with similar interests and hobbies. Smile, make a few complements or jokes, and, most importantly, be genuine! Remember, if a friendship doesn't work out, don't worry, and move on. There will be plenty of chances for you to make lasting relationships and integrate into your new high school. Good luck!

Warmly,
Eana
Community Ambassador

Dear Leader,

There are many ways to make new friends, even though it may seem scary! Find someone you have common interests with and start up a conversation with them! You could wait for someone to come to you, but it may take some time. Just remember that the most important thing is to be yourself and surround yourself with people who like you for you!

Racquel
Community Ambassador

Dear Leader,

I know moving to a new city and being the "new girl" can be really nerve-racking, especially when it seems like everyone is already adjusted. My advice to you is simply to be yourself and put yourself out there! Don't be afraid to start a conversation with someone. Introduce yourself and try talking about different hobbies, interests, and any similarities you might have. If you're too nervous to start a conversation outright, you can always try telling the person a joke, asking a question, or just complimenting them! You can naturally lead into a conversation afterwards. Joining clubs or sport teams is also another good way to make friends quickly with people you share an interest with!

When I was transitioning from middle school to high school, I was so nervous! Almost everyone at my high school knew each other because they all went to the same middle school together, but I went to a middle school in a different town. I was so scared that I wouldn't fit into any friend groups or make any friends. Luckily, I was able to meet my soon-to-be best friend on the first day! I remember walking in to my first class and being so nervous. I saw that the girl sitting next to me had a pencil case of my favorite show, and I decided to compliment her on it. We started talking about the show and after that, we started talking more and figured out we had the same schedule! We've been best friends ever since. Overall, just remember to take a deep breath and be yourself! It may take some time, but you will eventually find amazing friends and become adjusted to life in your new town and school.

Best of luck,
Samantha
Community Ambassador

🌧 *my thoughts*

_____

_____

_____

_____

_____

_____

_____

the transition

By Aubria King, *Write to Lead Intern*

<u>River Catholic High School</u>

The school bell aggressively echoed throughout the school cueing an immediate outpour of high school students from their classrooms. While to many the sound of the bell created a sense of excitement, the bell triggered my anxiety. My heartbeat quickened as I listened to the thunderous footsteps of my peers. The stale air suffocated me. I knew that in approximately 4.5 seconds my nightmare would begin. Clutching the straps of my pink Jansport backpack, I armed myself with the fake smile I practiced in the mirror the night before. I took one last look at the empty state of the classroom. Its humongous windows overlooked the towering trees surrounding my school's state of the art tennis court. I took a deep breath and stepped into the chaotic sea of students carrying the latest Louis Vuitton bags. I wondered what their houses looked like. Do they have massive walk-in closets for their countless name brand bags? Do they have a pool with a hot tub to compliment it? Do they—

An aggressive tug on my freshly braided hair interrupted my thought. My head jerked back, awakening a growing sense of anger within me. I turned my head to see the face of one of my fellow white classmates. Her face was pale, with an amused smile stretching across her face.

"When did your hair get so long?" Courtney said, twisting the ends of my box braids in her dainty, newly painted fingers.

When you are one of the only Black kids within your school, you tend to turn into their latest science experiment. I kindly snatched my braid, gave her my signature fake smile, and continued to trudge my way through hallways. I soothed myself with the thought of spring break beginning soon.

I finally reached the school door. I immediately saw my father's red minivan. He smiled at me and motioned for me to come over. I rushed to his car, looking both ways to make sure that no one saw me run to the nearly broken-down car. I was already one of the only Black kids in my school, I couldn't be seen riding in this.

"Welcome to Old Bessie," my dad said, slapping his hand across the side of the minivan. I immediately rolled my eyes. He refused to let go of this car. It's 2022, we literally have electric cars. I pray that the car does not break down each time we get in the car. The car sputtered for a few seconds and then took off. A deep sigh escaped my lips.

"Next stop, Aunt Crystal's house."

Aunt Crystal's House

The two-hour drive to my aunt's house was quiet. I pressed my face against the cool window and watched as the rural spaced-out houses blossomed into close knit, towering buildings. Empty roads became flooded with cars. The chorus of honking cars replaced the peaceful chirping of birds. My eyes did not leave the window once. I was simply in awe. This must be what they call "The City Life."

My dad had told me that we would be spending spring break at my aunt's house, but it had not occurred to me that her house was in the city. The last time I had seen my aunt was when I was a baby. Following my mom's passing, my dad had to work a lot more and never really had the time to take me to visit. This would be my first time visiting since I was one. After getting a glimpse of the city, my excitement shot through the roof.

Before I knew it, we were pulling up to a small, blue house on the corner. A petite woman sat on the porch, aggressively waving at the red van.

"Crystallllllllllllll!" my dad exclaimed.

My aunt immediately leaped from the steps and sprinted towards the minivan. She flung open the car door and rushed to embrace me. I was showered with a seemingly never-ending flow of hugs and kisses. Each kiss sent a warm shiver throughout my body. The feeling was foreign, but I loved it. She checked her watch, looked up at me and ushered me out of the car. It was nearing 4pm. It was time for her to pick my cousins up from school.

"Naomi, are you coming with me to pick up your cousins from school? They would love to see you," she said, already opening the passenger side door.

Although it seemed like she was asking me, her tone indicated that I didn't really have a choice. I hopped out of my dad's van and slid into my aunt's glistening silver Ford Explorer. Before I could blink, we arrived at a brick building. A big sign read, "Chestnut Ave School" plastered above two big blue doors. *This is their school?* My eyes thoroughly searched the simple brick building. No state-of-the-art tennis court? No swimming pool? All I could think about was how strange this all seemed.

Suddenly, an array of Black and brown students came bursting out of the school doors. I studied each and every student that walked out of the school doors. I saw box braids, cornrows, puffs, twists. Nobody was tugging their hair or questioning them. The students rushed out the building to socialize amongst themselves. Some girls played hand games, while others played tag or ran across the street to Double Dutch in the park. Desperate to elongate the moment, I took a picture. I never thought that a picture could have so much meaning and depth to it. As I admired the picture, my two cousins came running towards the car door.

"Hey Naomiiiiii!" Destiny and Desmond sang in perfect harmony. A smile formed on my lips. I was not expecting them to embrace me in such a welcoming manner. I mean they barely knew me. Within seconds, the car was filled with laughter and chatter. The bond was almost instant.

When we arrived at the house, Destiny and Desmond dragged me upstairs to their rooms. A warm draft of vanilla entered my nose. I looked around and immediately saw a wall full of posters. A range of Black faces lined the walls. Beyoncé. Martin Luther King. Kendrick Lamar. Quotes from Maya Angelou. Some of them I didn't even recognize.

Snap! One more picture couldn't hurt.

"Do you know who this is?" Destiny asked, pointing to a lady with a crown of locks, a string of pearls adorning her neck. Was this someone that I'm supposed to know? I slowly shook my head no. I didn't want to seem clueless, but I really wanted to know.

"This is Judge Ketanji Brown Jackson. She is the first Black female Justice in all of American history." A sense of pride swelled within Destiny as she said her name. It seemed to be contagious. Before we all knew it, a smile was on each of our faces. I pulled out my phone and began to Google her. Each fact awoke a sense of honor and pride within me. I felt like I was a part of her success. I felt empowered. Maybe one day I will be accomplishing something great.

I never really thought about my future before. I never thought about who I wanted to be and what road I wanted to take. The only plans I ever had was to attend an Ivy League college. Maybe Harvard. At my school, it was an expectation for everyone to attend an Ivy League. But honestly, I didn't even know a thing about Harvard.

"What college do you want to go to?" I found myself asking.

"SPELMAN and MOREHOUSE," the two sang.

"Spelman and Morehouse?" I questioned. Before I could even ask anything more, the two had already gone into a detailed presentation about the two schools.

"Morehouse and Spelman are sister and brother HBCUs in Atlanta, Georgia." From the look on my face, they could tell that I did not know what an HBCU was.

Desmond explained, "An HBCU is a Historically Black College, where many Black and brown students attend. It presents an alternative experience and education that heavily varies from an education at a PWI, a predominantly white institution."

An HBCU!? I made a mental note of this and added it to the list of things that I needed to google tonight.

Destiny ran to the speaker and pressed play. A mixture of Beyoncé, Frank Ocean, Kendrick Lamar, and some artists I didn't know existed played in rotation. I had about ten songs to google by dinner time.

During dinner, an array of dishes was placed on the table. Turkey wings, mac and cheese, cabbage, and cornbread. My mouth began watering. I love my father, but this was certainly better than his cooking. My plate had absolutely no crumbs left when I finished.

The next day, Destiny and Desmond decided to take me with them to go hang out with their friends. Without question, they immediately embraced me and welcomed me into their friend group. There were no cliques, no eliteness, just genuine and accepting people. I was nearly hesitant to accept their affection. I had never experienced this before.

But what I did not realize was how intense their debates over political and social issues were. They discussed microaggressions, internalized racism, issues within the Black community itself. I admired the way in which they were so educated on the world, socially aware and how they articulated themselves so well. I, in fact, was a tad bit embarrassed by the fact that I did not know as much as they did. I made several more notes of things I wanted to research when we got back home. Before the end of the day, I made sure I took a picture with them.

The week flew by. Each day was a day encompassed by new experiences and new things for me to learn. I never realized how little I knew about myself or my culture.

The day of departure, I found myself saddened to know that I wouldn't have access to these talks and experiences anymore. As I collected all my toiletries from the bathroom, I looked in the mirror. I admired my cocoa brown complexion and the smoothness of it. It made me smile. That same feeling of pride awoke within me once again. Before I left the bathroom I took a picture in the mirror, to hold onto this feeling for as long as I could. However, I had a feeling that it was not going away.

The Return

The whole ride home I talked to my dad about everything that I learned and saw. I did not leave a single detail out. From the rear-view mirror, I saw a slight smile form on my dad's face. I pulled out my phone once again and took a picture.

Monday morning, it was time for me to go to school again. I spent the whole car ride staring at the pictures that I took over the past week. This time I walked boldly through my school doors. Courtney quickly ran up to me to see what hairstyle I had today. When she reached up to touch my hair, I took a smooth step to the side.

"Please do not touch my hair without my permission." I gave her a smile and continued to go about my day.

Today is going to be a great day.

journal: *Why was Naomi able to find her voice and stand up to Courtney after visiting her cousins? Have you ever struggled to find your voice? If so, what made speaking up difficult?*

_____

_____

_____

_____

_____

_____

_____

_____

_____

_____

_____

_____

_____

_____

_____

_____

_____

_____

YOGA FOR THE COMMUNITY:
A CANDID INTERVIEW WITH JYLL HUBBARD SALK

BY KOUDJEDJI COULIBALY

KOUDJEDJI:
Okay, so the first few questions will be about connecting with yourself. And so the first question is, how would you define yoga?

JYLL:
Yoga, basically, is the connection of the mind, body, and the spirit. For me, yoga is movement. Asana is when you're moving into a posture. Then you breathe, which is gamma, which is your breath. And then it's just spirit. So for me, it's all of that. My yoga is beyond my mat. Yoga is my life. Does that answer your question, hun?

KOUDJEDJI:
Yeah, that makes so much sense. Thank you for telling me that. When I first think of yoga, I just think of stretching and doing all of that stuff. I never thought it was anything that deep.

So the second question is, why did you name your studio, Urban Asanas?

JYLL:
So Asana is posture, and the Sanskrit word for yoga, or in yoga. Urban is because I'm in the hood of Brooklyn. So Hood, Hood, you know. I'm a Black woman and Urban Asanas is the only Black-owned Yoga Studio in my hood.

KOUDJEDJI:
That's really cool. Because I feel like there are so many stereotypes about the hood, that it makes people not want to come. People think about gang violence or something unsafe, and that's not true.

JYLL:
I mean, I'm here. The good stuff is here. I love my neighborhood. I love it. I love the people who come into my place.

KOUDJEDJI:
That's really cool. I'm nervous.

JYLL:
Don't be nervous, honey, just take your time. I'm here. I am honored. I am truly honored that you're doing this with me. So take your time.

JYLL HUBBARD SALK

You got to take care of yourself. You can't pour from an empty cup. You have to make sure that you take care of yourself.

KOUDJEDJI:
Thank you. Okay, so have you ever done collaborations with any other yoga studio companies?

JYLL:
I've done collaborations with other wellness spaces and businesses. You know what I mean? My girlfriend, she has a meditation place and she sells a lot of CBD things and crystals. She and I have collaborated on things of that nature, anything that's anything with well-being, I'm collaborating on. But also it's hard to collaborate now since we're still in the middle of a pandemic.

KOUDJEDJI:
Thank you so much for that. You mentioned a girlfriend. Do you identify as queer?

JYLL:
Girlfriend as in friend. I'm not queer. But my younger self might be, you know. (laughs) Way back. I'm 55 years old, and I got three babies. I've been married for 25 years. I've done more than you've done in your life. I've lived in New York for 30 years. So I know the ins and outs of everything. We're gonna leave it at that!

KOUDJEDJI:
Okay, so we're gonna go on to the next section of questions. Okay, so, what does family mean to you?

JYLL:
Security. I have three daughters, my mom and my husband, and my brother who lives in Connecticut with his husband. My family is my go to—my safe space. I mean, even though they get on my nerves. I can't stand my daughters sometimes. But they got me. That's family.

KOUDJEDJI:
I relate to that. So much. I can't stand my siblings either. But without them...

JYLL:
Yeah, that's what it is.

KOUDJEDJI:

So what is the longest friendship you ever had? Your longest friendships?

JYLL:

You really want to know?

KOUDJEDJI:

Yes.

JYLL:

My relationship with me. Because I've had to be with myself for 55 years.

KOUDJEDJI:

I love that.

JYLL:

I came in alone. I'm going out alone. You know what I mean? So I have to always nurture and take care of Jyll... As much as I'm an extrovert and I got this big personality, I love to be by myself. I love to be alone.

KOUDJEDJI:

Yeah, but I just really love what you said. I didn't even expect that answer. But that was amazing. I need to think about myself too. I'm always trying to put other people first and it never works.

JYLL:

Oh, don't do that. Stop doing that. Don't do that. You got to take care of yourself. You can't pour from an empty cup. You have to make sure that you take care of yourself.

KOUDJEDJI:

Yes, I will. This is the last part. So it's connecting with community. So what does community mean to you?

JYLL:

I'm in Crown Heights in Brooklyn, so community to me is diversity. Where I am there is a heavy West Indian community. Now with the gentrification, white people are kind of moving into the neighborhood, and moving the Black people out. But it seems some of the ones that are moving in, are really trying to keep the bones of this community. And so that's what's important to me. With my yoga studio, I always say, I want Ta'Quanda to be able to practice next to Becky, you know what I mean? So that is my community. I make sure that my joint's diverse. I want everybody. No judgment. I want people to feel safe. That's important to me.

journal: *Jyll talks about the importance of having a good relationship with herself, her family, and her community. Which relationships do you value the most? Why?*

_____

_____

_____

_____

_____

_____

_____

_____

_____

_____

_____

_____

_____

_____

_____

_____

_____

_____

_____

repairing mother-daughter relationships

Dear Cocoon Club,

My mom and I used to be so close but now it's a struggle to even have a conversation without arguing, plus she's always working or stressed out about something. What could I do to repair our relationship and bond?

cocoon club responses

Dear Leader,

I think it's best that you schedule a time to talk with your mom to express how you feel. Sometimes work is stressful; it can get the best of us and start to consume our good energy. I believe having an honest conversation is the most effective way to communicate what's going on. Open the discussion by saying something like, "Hey Mom, I feel like we're growing distant from one another. Can we talk before the day is over?" This offers a safe space to be honest about the origin of your tension. However, talking it out can be a bit too daunting of a task for some people. An alternative can be planning an activity to spend time with each other. This could be something as effortless as playing a game together or watching a movie. Quality time could ease the tension because you both are engaged in something fun together. I think your mom needs some peace of mind, and I'm sure that you can help give that to her.

Natalie
Community Ambassador

Dear Leader,

I would say that taking time to reflect could be most important here. Since you've already tried the communication approach, taking time to reflect on your mother's situation and trying to understand her perspective on things may make it easier for you to communicate with your mother. Also, try asking her if she's able to take the time to listen to the struggles you've gone through because of all your arguing. I hope this helps.

Madison
Community Ambassador

Dear Leader,

It is commendable that you are willing to put in the effort to repair your relationship. I would recommend playing a board game, watching a movie, or partaking in an activity that you two enjoy doing together. A lot of teen girls in our Cocoon Club find these things are great bonding activities. In this way, your mom can relieve some stress and the two of you can have some fun together. Having an activity planned also gives some structure to where your conversation will go, making talking easier. When you feel comfortable you can also start a discussion with her with something like, "Spending time with you has been nice. I've noticed you've been stressed lately. Is everything ok?" Having a discussion when both of you are more relaxed can be incredibly helpful for your relationship.

Asmi
Community Ambassador

protect and serve

By Rashanna James-Frison, *Write to Lead Intern*

Walking down 18th Ave, I hear car horns blaring up and down the street. Despite being used to such an environment, I can't help but be at least a bit irritated. Bright headlights fly up and down the avenue, providing at least some sort of illumination. It's around 6:45 at night so it's getting dark, but there's still many people out. I am on my way to the store just to get something to eat; I have on my coat and a hood, to keep myself warm. I'm listening to H.E.R, volume at a decent level. As I'm walking, I see lights, and not no Christmas lights, like you would think so, but it was police lights.

The police car stops beside me, and my only thoughts right then are, "What did I do?" "Why is the police stopping me?" I take out my headphones and ask politely,

"Is there a problem officer?"

"What are you doing out late, at this time of night?"

"It's only 9pm, sir," I chuckle.

"Answer the question," he says with a straight face. His weird mustache and shades make him even more intimidating. I realize he is not joking. I quickly remove my smile and answer.

"I'm just going to the store to get something to eat," I say, fidgeting with my hands in my pocket. The wind is howling and my body feels like it's going to freeze up any second. My mama always told me stories about the police, so being in this predicament goes to show she wasn't lying.

"Oh yeah, what's in your pocket?" he asks snidely.

"My hands sir," I stutter a little.

"Let me see, your hands," making a gesture towards my coat.

As of right now, people are starting to come out to see what is going on. Some are recording the whole thing.

"I don't have anything, sir," I say, looking at everyone, being too scared to move.

"I said, let me see your hands," he demands as he gets out of the car.

I am beyond scared at this point; I start stepping back as he gets closer to where he is towering over me. As I do, I bump into someone, I look back to see my older brother. I let out a breath of relief.

"Thank God," I say to myself.

"Is there a problem, officer?" he asks, wrapping his arms around me. He is taller than me and buff; he played basketball when he was in high school, so he kept that body shape from working out. The officer looks at him then me.

"No, there isn't. I was just asking why she was out at this time of night," he replies. He retreats back to the police car.

The officer pulls off, a few seconds later.

I turn around and hug my brother so hard, shaking because of the situation.

"It's ok, I'm here," he reassures me.

We walk back to the house, holding one another. Once we are at the house, I let go of him so he could open the door. I rush upstairs, ready to tell my mama everything that just happened, but she is asleep. I go into my brother's room, and ask him,

"How did you know?"

"Ms. Jackson, told me. She saw you, with the police, talking to you. You know I don't play with you, so I ran out to get you," he replies.

"Thank you big bro, I don't know what would have happened if you didn't come in time." I say truthfully.

"Of course, little sis, I love you. Now get some sleep," he says.

"Ok, see you in the morning," I reply.

I walk into my room, and flop on the bed. Next thing you know, I'm asleep.

I wake up, to the sight of the police officer standing over me.

"Thought you were gonna get away, didn't you?"

I scream and jump up.

"Wait... it was just a dream," I say panting.

journal: *Several police departments in the United States have the motto "to protect and to serve." Do you feel protected and served by police? Why or why not? Who protects and serves your community?*

_____

_____

_____

_____

_____

_____

_____

_____

_____

_____

_____

_____

_____

_____

_____

_____

_____

_____

_____

_____

i always wanted to be the sun.

to have warmth and light follow wherever I travel

to have everything i touch be illuminated with my light

to be what draws everyone to their consciousness

a driving force that calls the earth to action

but the moon is what calls the earth to rest

shining its brightest when no one's around

a lone figure in the sky

with rays not bright enough to demand the attention

sometimes full, at its best

but sometimes small enough to disappear into the night

i'm more like the moon.

but the sun cannot shine without the moon

as the moon cannot wax or wane without the sun

after all, the sun is what illuminates the moon at night.

By Kiara Casseus, *Cocoon Club Member*

flying towards the moon

By Janae Wilson, *Write to Lead Intern*

I lost my ring, ring to my Saturn; that made me who I am, and what keeps me sad. I, Veria Griffin, was the quiet and productive one: having a healthy connection with my sister, having good grades, and a decent life. Unlike my oldest sister Zimira, who tended to be the outgoing one: being more popular, going out more, and being more adventurous. Zi had always been an impact to the community; starting food drives, donating to charity, and so much more. She was the golden child. She helped others to the point where she forgot about me, her other half, and it hurt. But an enormous meteor came crashing out of the sky. I didn't see it coming. December 31 was the day I lost my ring and all the stars fell out of my universe.

December 31, 2011

My sister said that she was going over to one of her friend, Vixen's, house when she was supposed to be with me to see the blue moon together. I was just so mad because she once again backed out from our plans to go to another stupid party. I know I should not have, yet I got her grounded. But did that stop her from sneaking out? Nope. Due to the dramatic increase of gun violence, I began to get worried. I held on to my locket, the ones my mother got us when we were seven. Zi's being a silver rocket and mine being a rose gold heart that opened and had an engraving on one side saying, "Forever and always." The other side has space for a tiny picture, but I can never find a picture small enough. After calming my nerves, I headed towards Vixen's house myself.

On the way there I saw Zimira. I went up to her and asked, "Where were you?"

"I got bored. Why do you care anyway? You're the one who got me grounded."

"We had plans and you bailed on me to be with your friend again like you always do."

"I don't always bail on you."

"Yes, you do. Whenever I try to hang out with you, you bail and go hang out with Vixen. It's like you're ashamed of me—"

"I'm not ashamed."

"Yes, you are, and if you're so embarrassed by me then don't even talk to me."

I storm off not saying anything else. Twenty minutes passed, and we were close to the house. I was about to open the door when I heard cars screeching and guns shooting. Zimira grabs me and ducks us out of fear and sits still until there is no sound. Hearing whispers from the neighbors lowers my guard, and I turn around to let Zimira know that it's ok, but she is not moving.

Salty tears fall down my cheeks in disbelief. My heart continuously thumps; I can hear it in my ears. The murmur from my neighbors becomes distant below me and my sister's corpse. My quivering hands are stained with Zi's blood. Despair washes over my face, and I hear my mother open the door and see my sister's dead body on the floor and broken screams are released from her throat as she comes to the realization. Zimira saved me; even when we were mad at each other she had decided to save me. My knees fall, heavy water droplets start descending from the sky fulfilling this dark and depressing scene, and my mother continues crying for God to bring her back. It all makes me even more broken. With the little strength I had left I looked up and the moon turned purple.

February 4, 2014

Three years after Zimira's death, Ma and I still haven't gotten over Zi. After her death, the crime ratings had dropped down from 87% to 29% making the area a little safer. Multiple donations, from the people Zi helped before her death, helped pay for her funeral making my mom's life barely better after losing one of her daughters. Even after we moved from that neighborhood, her presence is still around us almost like she is watching over us as a way of protection.

Ma went to church every day since the incident hoping that Zimira is at peace wherever she is and as a coping method from it. I, on the other hand, am working on my Master's in Engineering and Biological Sciences at Harvard on a full scholarship. Holding on to the locket, releasing the stress due to midterms coming up, I sit here and wonder. Can I become an astronaut or is everything I'm doing pointless? Zi and I did everything together; we sang together, did blogs together, LIVED together, and we were supposed to become astronauts together. But ever since that day, the dreams we built together felt dead without her, and the moon always stayed that hauntingly indigo color.

March 2, 2015

Going through the boxes with expired memories brings pain to my heart. Our smiles, hopes, and dreams, so unaware of the catastrophic ending that was bound to happen. This doesn't help me. I need to hear her voice. I found a videotape labeled "The Saturn Sisters: Saturday Night Live." *I don't remember this*. My curiosity got the best of me, and I played it. There were two eleven-year-olds, dressed in professional clothes, at an old desk, with a cardboard sign reading "Saturn Sisters: Saturday Night Live, **Featuring Veria and Zimira Griffin.**" Now I remember. We used to make videos about the space for our mom when she was at work.

"Hello, young stars my name is Veria—"

"I'm Zimira."

"—and we are the Saturn Sisters here to tell you about life beyond the universe."

It's just like her to interrupt me and take the spotlight. God, I miss her so much.

"Today we are going to talk about the Divine Pairing. It's an urban legend that whenever there is something tremendous in the world it has always come down to two people and to restore balance one has to be sacrificed."

Zermia saved me even when we were mad at each other. She had decided to save me.

"Purple moon symbolizes a sacrifice needed to restore the balance."

"What is something so bad that requires a sacrifice?" Younger me asks.

"I don't know but probably something where a death means justice or an acknowledgment."

"What if we become a Divine Pairing and one of us has to die?" Younger me questions while clutching onto the necklace in fear of what might happen.

It pains me to know the answer now.

"Nothing will happen to us, Veria. Even if one of us has to leave, the plan stays the same. We will become astronauts and become the first generation of Griffin sisters in space, even if one didn't make it."

I cut the video off and tears fall from my face. I say to myself, "I'm sorry Zi, you were right. You are still here in spirit, and I will do this for you."

<u>March 16, 2021</u>

Ten years of tears, stress, and hard work, here I am getting ready to go to my spaceship. As I am getting ready to leave my mom's house, it's closer to NASA than my apartment, and I am pulled into a bone-crushing hug.

"I'm so proud of you, Veria," my mom says.

"I know Ma, thank you."

"Everything is going to be okay, kiddo," Andrew says. Andrew Phillips is my mom's new husband, and she gave birth six years ago to my little brother, Julian. I am so happy my mom found some happiness in her life.

"And Veria, before I forget, here is a picture of you and Zi together when y'all was sixteen. I tried to make the picture as small as I could so it can fit in your locket so you can take it in space with you."

While she was speaking, I couldn't help but look at the photo; it was taken four months before the shooting. The last photo of us together.

"Th-thank you mo-mom," I managed to say while trembling. I wipe away the last of my tears as I hug them for the last time before leaving.

Sitting in this spacecraft, with four others each wearing twenty pounds of materials, waiting for this long and desired mission: to be the first Griffin to go to the moon. If only Zimira was here to experience it with me.

After the countdown, one of the other scientists presses the launch button. Feeling huge amounts of force being pressed against me, we break earth barriers and go towards the moon.

Three days after the launch, we open the spacecraft, unpack everything, and start to move towards the moon base. Successfully moving everything to the base, we start our mission. Before I start planting potatoes in the garden, I start to appreciate the sight in front of me: the rocky texture of the moon, the darkness of the universe only getting light by the burning of the stars in it, and lastly, the image of the other planets. But the earth is the most beautiful, with the dark blue armor surrounding it as a whole, and a light tint of gray clouds hovering over Africa and Europe. It is breathtaking. Clutching the locket calms my over-wrecking nerves as I can feel the presence of her, even though I'm far away from earth.

"We did it, Zi. We did it," I say quietly, not knowing if she could hear me. But almost instantly I hear a familiar ghostly voice saying,

"We did, didn't we, Veria," and I turn around hoping to see that person, but I don't. Yet her voice alone puts my mind at ease as I turn around and finally start my work, sensing her no longer around me. The moon is no longer purple.

journal: *Have you ever experienced the death of a loved one? If so, how do you stay connected to your loved one's spirit and the memories you shared? How do you honor their life?*

_____

_____

_____

_____

_____

_____

_____

_____

_____

_____

_____

_____

_____

_____

_____

_____

_____

_____

_____

_____

MANUFACTURING LEADERSHIP: TY MCCULLOUGH

BY AUTUMN EVANS

When you think of a leader, you think of a person that inspires you, someone that can guide you, and someone who can give you the best advice. When evaluating these attributes, I think of one of my close mentors, Ty McCullough. Ty McCullough, who is in the leadership division of her manufacturing job, is a hands-on, supportive, lead-by-example mentor who allows people and young girls to become leaders in whatever they do.

Before starting the interview process, I went through the people in my life. I wanted to choose someone who would be the best person to be a role model in leadership. I wanted to choose someone who had a long line of making sure that girls are empowered as they develop leadership skills. After careful consideration, I picked Ty McCullough because I have worked closely with her through the College Application Process (CAP) program through Alpha Kappa Alpha. After working with her, I instantly knew that she had many of the qualities of a leader.

When speaking to Ty McCullough, she was a bit nervous about the interview because no one asked her about her job from an in-depth perspective. We started casually to ease into the discussion, and I didn't start with the fundamental questions. I began by asking about her passion. I discovered that she loves using her skills and love for her work to inspire others. I found that she is passionate about making an impact on African American girls, teens, and young women to encourage them to seek careers in STEM.

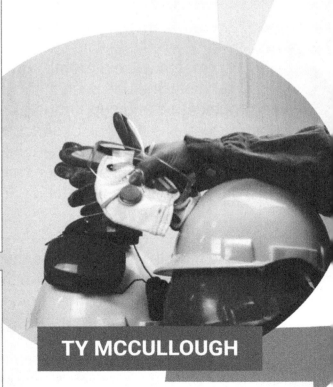

TY MCCULLOUGH

She is an effective leader because she shares her experience and education to build successful teams.

In her current role as an automotive manufacturing lead, she is responsible for the following:
- Team of 50 individuals
- Establish goals and recommendations for the team to build the company
- Shares feedback to the team
- Ensures that product lines are manufactured accurately and safely

She is an effective leader because she shares her experience and education to build successful teams. She is supportive and works with her team and helps them grow and develop in their careers, and promotes personal career growth. She accomplishes this through open communication, listening to her teams' goals and aspirations, and helping them develop a plan for success. She says she is inspired by other female leaders such as Justice Ruth Bader Ginsburg, Ava DuVernay, and Michelle Obama. She stated one quote from Justice Ginsburg that I admire, "Fight for the things that you care about, but do it in a way that will lead others to join you."

Ty McCullough is an exceptional leader and a great mentor. In her role, she inspires others with her style of leadership. Ty shared that she works in a male-dominated field and uses critical skills regularly. I have observed that one of her best traits is that she exudes confidence. She is an effective communicator, has mastered emotional intelligence, and uses critical thinking to solve problems. She is also a visionary and has learned how to solicit ideas from her team. She meets weekly with her entire team to discuss short and long-term goals in this role.

She also meets twice a month with employees to discuss personal success and opportunities. She has been in this role for 20 years. She finds that consistent communication and support help develop a successful team and shows that what she does or learns is the type of success she wants to instill in her group. She also thinks of her team as her family. When she thinks of her team, she treats them like a family and sets high standards for her work family; she has incorporated the style of modeling as an example to lead.

We know female leaders across the globe have a wealth of knowledge – lessons they've learned throughout their careers. Too often, African American female leaders are scrutinized, ridiculed; their leadership is questioned and many times they've been made to feel as though they are less accomplished. We all watched the highly qualified Judge Ketanji Brown Jackson confirmation hearings, and many women in leadership roles can relate to how her qualifications were questioned. Ty McCullough has successfully used skills she has learned and experienced to become a highly effective leader.

journal: *Ty is an exceptional leader and mentor. She develops and supports her team, while still encouraging them to achieve high standards. What role do you usually play on a team? Why?*

_____

_____

_____

_____

_____

_____

_____

_____

_____

_____

_____

_____

_____

_____

_____

_____

_____

_____

friendships & dating

Let's Connect: Have you ever had to have a difficult conversation with a friend about a person she was dating or interested in?

my thoughts

thoughts from the cocoon club:

"The conversation with my friend was difficult because she didn't see everything everyone else saw. She didn't see the narcissism, the gas lighting, or manipulation. Because she looked at him differently, she had more faith in him and what he'd tell her, instead of considering what everyone else was warning her about."

—Kenaisia, *ExCEL Fellow*

I had a friend who was dating her first boyfriend. During this span of time, she would vent her concerns about him, and from her stories, I felt several red flags arise. One of the biggest was her being inexperienced and him not explaining proper protection measures to her. At one point during one of their "breaks," he had intimate relations with another girl, but lied to my friend that he did not. He only revealed it to her when that girl tested positive for an STI, and he had to tell my friend so that she could get tested too. This was the point where I felt that I should have a meaningful conversation with her.

Because of the on and off nature of their relationship, it was difficult to talk to her about breaking up with him for real. She would always start the conversation that she wanted to, but it would become a cycle of them breaking up and getting back together. The most difficult part was that it got to the point where trying to be there for her in this situation was too exhausting as a friend. She would bring him up in every conversation, ask for and agree with our advice, and then do the opposite. It was having such a harmful effect on our friendship that I needed to tell her that I didn't want to talk to her about him anymore if she had no intentions of changing anything. Doing so healed our relationship, but I wish that it didn't have to get to that point.

—Jade, *ExCEL Fellow*

journal: What are some challenges that a teen girl may face when her and/or her friends start dating?

- **peer pressure:** being coerced by others to drink, smoke, have sex (virginity shaming), etc.

- **change in energy:** her friends may distance themselves (she may distance herself). She may feel alone and outcasted, changing how she and her friends interact with each other.

- **unbalanced relationships:** feeling like she needs to do everything in a relationship to keep it going while her partner does nothing.

—Kenaisia

- a more experienced partner who may be teaching her things that are not safe, too fast, blatantly wrong, etc.

- a physically abusive partner

- a cheating partner

—Jade

lead the way: *Sometimes it's hard to figure out how to talk to our friends or partners about dating. Think about the challenges you listed on the previous page.* **What would you say** *in each situation? What* **wouldn't** *you say?*

what to say *by Kenaisia*

peer pressure

- *"Ask one another if doing this now changes the way you feel for one another. If your partner cannot love you because you don't want to do certain things that you are not ready for, or simply don't want to do, then the relationship may not be worth it after all."*

- *"Tell your partner what you're ready for as you grow into your relationship. Don't just say yes and agree because you don't want the person to get mad or break up with you. You'll regret doing anything you don't want to do."*

change in energy

- *"Tell your friend you miss them—that you barely see each other, and you miss spending time together."*

- *"Ask to schedule a girls' day or find an activity you can do together."*

unbalanced relationships

- *"Tell your partner you want to do more, that you need more from them. A relationship isn't one sided."*

- *"Set and communicate your boundaries and requirements; make it clear that you want your love language to be communicated."*

my thoughts

What NOT to say
by Kenaisia

- *"Yes"* when you really want to say *"no"* or you're not sure.

- *"You got you a little relationship, now you think you're somebody"* or anything along the lines of being disrespectful or hating.

- *"It's okay"* or *"That's fine with me"* when in reality, it isn't. Tell the person how you really feel, what you're comfortable and uncomfortable with. Don't be afraid to tell someone your needs and wants.

what to say *by Jade*

the experienced partner

- Start by mentioning something the partner said that was wrong and showing some form of proof. It is important to maintain a casual and nonjudgmental tone so that the friend is open to whatever is being shown to them.

- "Hey ____, last time I remember you telling me that [partner] told you _____. I was a little confused about that so I actually looked it up and this is what I found."

the physically abusive partner

- Talk gently and reassure the friend that you are just concerned about their safety; be careful not to say anything that can be misconstrued as it being her fault.

- "Hi ____, I saw some bruises on your arm and it's not the first time I've seen them. I'm concerned for your safety. If you don't feel comfortable talking to me it's okay. I just want you to know that I'm here for you, and nothing is your fault. Always feel free to talk to me whether it's now or in the future."

the cheating partner

- Remain objective when presenting the evidence, be supportive of her reaction, and if the "evidence" is unclear, remind the friend that she should confirm with the partner to avoid any misunderstandings.

- "Hi ____, I heard/saw something that you might want to sit down for. I think that [partner] might be cheating on you. I'm pretty sure I saw [partner] kissing Girl A in the locker room the other day. I think you should ask [partner] about it to make sure it's not a misunderstanding, but I thought it was best to let you know in case it's not."

my thoughts

What NOT to say *by Jade*

- "[Friend], you need to break up with [partner]. They're terrible and teaching you wrong things and I don't think you should be with them."

- "I saw what [partner] did to you. I can't believe you'd even be with someone like that. If you stay with them, then you deserve what you get."

- "[Friend], guess what. I heard [partner] was alone with Girl A in the locker room. You better not forgive them."

INTERVIEW WITH TAHNIA ROGERS:
YOGA, MOTHERHOOD, + BALANCE

BY JASMINE SAINT LOUIS

TAHNIA ROGERS

Keep on going and focus on your goals, and everything else will fall into place.

I have gotten the unique opportunity to interview businesswoman Tahnia Rogers. She is a woman who seems to have her life organized beautifully for her busy lifestyle. Tahnia Rogers owns the business, The Roots Studio, created to offer yoga classes to the general public to educate and heal the collective. The business life for Tahnia is extremely fulfilling since she gets to do what she loves every day.

Although new to motherhood, Tahnia still pursues her passion for yoga with persistence and love. Through her superior organizational skills and drive, Tahnia has built her yoga business and maintained it to showcase her abilities to the community. Tahnia tries her best to showcase her lifestyle and promote her business in the best, most attractive light for potential customers and brands when it comes to social media. Though she struggles to maintain a consistent social media presence, her company continues to thrive, and she has a goal to improve her presence online as the days come.

Tahnia's love for yoga keeps her feeling balanced in all aspects of her life. She seeks to share her expertise in yoga with the world to spread love and balance because these are the positive qualities yoga brings to her life. She has an eye for problems that can be solved in her community and tries her best to solve them with her available resources. Tahnia knows how much yoga has improved her life and feels that if people did yoga every day, their world would be a much more understanding and calming place. She's always willing to extend a helping hand to the community in any way she can.

She is an extremely helpful individual who will take the time to help anyone out. Tahnia takes pride in her community, and she truly wants to see the people in her community do better for themselves, as well as for others. Aside from yoga, Tahnia loves to travel and experience life. As most businesswomen do, she feels it is best to put work first before personal life; however, work is her passion, so she does not have an issue with this. Since Tahnia believes strongly in keeping a balance in everything she does, she does her best to make time for her personal life.

Even as a hardworking woman, Tahnia still loves her family, so she enjoys coming home when the work is done and spending her free time with them. Since Tahnia is pregnant right now, she feels that her work life and personal life are a little more challenging since she barely has the energy to work as hard as she used to. Being pregnant with her first child, she has taken on the mommy role while balancing her work life. Fortunately, Tahnia has people she can lean on when she's struggling. She believes that it is essential to have a support system as a working woman.

Tahnia feels blessed to have a husband she can always come home to who doesn't expect all of her attention because he understands how hardworking she is. Tahnia believes it is best to have people, like her husband, around her who encourage her to pursue her passions and are there for her when she is having trouble or needing a break from being a businesswoman. Balancing her work life and personal life may be hard at this time, but Tahnia uses resources like a support system, alarms, and yoga to keep her on track and focus on her goals. She feels it's best to keep on going and focus on your goals, and everything else will fall into place exactly how it needs to with persistence.

journal: *One of the ways Tahnia strives to maintain balance is by having a strong and encouraging support system. What kind of people do you want in your support system? Why?*

_____

_____

_____

_____

_____

_____

_____

_____

_____

_____

_____

_____

_____

_____

_____

_____

_____

_____

_____

A Letter to My Father that He Will Never Read

I ran to my mother with feather steps that gave me jitters and a clamminess I'll never forget; she was bleached in tears. My 7-year-old mind was not ready, it was not ready to face a harsh reality. My mother sat in the corner of the room with a startled expression I can only hope to never see again.

It scared me whenever one of my parents cried. Maybe he was going on a vacation for a few days, maybe he would be relaxed and at peace there. Maybe the sun would shine, and he would come back a better dad. I was thinking through all the "what if's" and "maybe's" when it came to the dreaded moment.

He was leaving for good. I realized this as I watched my mother weep, as I asked her what was wrong. One quick hug from him and a closed front door later, I realized I would no longer have a real father. There was no man of the family that could carry me on those broad, strong shoulders. Those shoulders of his were supposed to be supportive of the "burden" that came with raising three children. They presumably carried our life and money, but that was just the way I was taught to think. I was supposed to have a normal family.

I didn't.

Who did, though? My dad. Alone was a good family for him, perhaps. He was free of the pressure of keeping the family safe and sound. Safe and sound meant money, it meant that he had to make money to support us. The day before his forever departure, I helped him pack. A plaid dress shirt, green and blue, smelled like the ocean. It had a smell of eucalyptus and fresh crystalline salt. I envied that smell; it was so beautiful. Every now and then I catch a hint of that exact smell on my mother. I forget she still uses that essence on her clothing. I refuse to go near enough to smell it now. Unless I have to.

She doesn't need to add any of that smell on her clothes from a few years back, it was already drenched into each knot of fabric. Just like my father was.

I know that my dad still loves me. I feel it when we speak on the phone, and he urges me to turn on video. He wants to see my face, to see what it looks like, to see if I resemble him. I wish he would see what became of my life, not my face. I wanted him to cherish something more important than how "beautiful" I turned out. I wanted him to cherish me. The person I became, the accomplishments I've made. How far I've gone.

I remember how you held my and as we walked through the crowds of Times Square, lights flashing everywhere, dancers running and twirling with the wind. I remember that it was my first time using the New York city subway; you took out noise-canceling headphones because I was afraid of the beeps and honks. You would pick me up from the school bus stop every day, with no lateness at *all, and give me kisses and hugs as soon as you saw me. I remember being afraid that you would be squashed if you fell into the train tracks. Funny how I wasn't afraid that I would fall into the tracks. I held onto you for dear life because I was your protector, but first you protected me.*

I remember hiking, and we came across a rocky path that ran downwards. The wind was whispering and told me that I was to fall with just a few pebbles blowing away from the bunch. I knew I was to fall, but I did not move. I did not breathe. Silence. Maybe you read my expression or maybe you knew me too well. You pulled me into those shoulders of safety, and suddenly I was okay.

Our memories evoke feelings of hatred, despair, grief, and so much more. In some strange way, though, they seem to remind me of how far I've come. Each moment, regardless of the good or the bad, has allowed me to get where I am today, to become the person I am now. I love you, dad. But I hate you for leaving. I still cannot answer the only question I have for you, why? Perhaps you will never answer it. But maybe I can help you, maybe I can pull you into my shoulders of knowledge. Not now, but soon. I don't know when it will be soon, but I promise to try, and I will make sure you don't forget. Because I won't ever forget the feeling of you giving me kisses and playing all the princess games I wanted to try. I won't forget clipping your hair into braids that I embedded with colorful scraps of post-its. Perhaps your hair will be white and thinned and old when I see you again. But I won't forget, and neither will you. I'll make sure you don't. I love you, I love you, I love you.

By Eana Shah, *Community Ambassador*

red light. green light

Let's Connect: *Have you ever ignored red or green flags while dating or getting to know someone?*

💭 *my thoughts*

thoughts from the cocoon club:

I was in a relationship with a guy named Jack (this isn't the real person's name). In this relationship, Jack made me feel like I took too much of his time and was overall a clingy person. He said he didn't trust me because "I would never trust females." Then when I felt some type of way, he would make it seem like it was my fault. Therefore (after a while), I left him, but I still kept in contact with him. Jack at times would laugh and make fun of the way he treated me. He even went as far as saying the hurt he brought me built me up, and he knew that he was going to be the one to do that in my life. One of the biggest red flags I didn't see was when he would tell me about his player moves and his ideology on women.

—**Amber,** *ExCEL Fellow*

The red flags that I ignored while I was dating someone at one point was how ineffective their communication was and how emotionally detached they were.

—**Naema,** *ExCEL Fellow*

For many years, I was attracted to "potential" over real progress—meaning I was more attracted to who a guy "could be" than who he actually was. During this time, I ignored green flags or "good guys" who actually had their stuff together (e.g., guys who made good grades, cared about similar interests as me, showed genuine interest in me, etc.).

—**Joy,** *ExCEL Instructor*

While dating at a young age, being naive and "in love" will make you ignore many red flags. Some red flags I ignored in past relationships include treating their mother badly along with other women in public, not tipping at restaurants, gaslighting, and not accepting my feelings on certain things that bothered me. In relationships at a young age, it can also be hard to see flags because boys and girls are still maturing and may not know how to treat each other. At first sight of seeing red flags, people should decide if continuing with the relationship would be better than dealing with constant red flags in a partner, outweighing the good versus the bad they bring.

—Natasha, *ExCEL Fellow*

journal: *What are some* **red flags** *that you think teen girls should be mindful of when dating or getting to someone?*

- *Strong negative reactions to minor inconveniences (ex: anger when having to reschedule a date)*
- *Constantly projecting "perfect" traits onto partner (ex: "I know you would never be so _____", or "that's my _____ girl")*
- *Disrespecting boundaries and pressuring to move quickly (especially when the pressuring partner is more experienced with dating)*
- *Talking negatively about others (especially friends) behind their back*
- *Treating staff/workers poorly*
- *Treating their partner differently when alone vs. when with friends (especially if trying to look "cool" in front of friends)*

—Jade

- *Possessiveness*
- *Projection of insecurity*
- *Too dependent*
- *Too nonchalant*
- *Making you choose between them and your loved ones*

—Naema

- *A lot of flirty/inappropriate comments on their social media*
- *Makes you feel like you're wrong for feeling the way you do*
- *Tells you to get rid of your friends or begins to isolate you*
- *Feels insecure about the things you wear or makes you feel less confident*
- *Doesn't see a future with you*

—Amber

lead the way: *What are some **green flags** that you think teen girls should be mindful of when dating or getting to someone?*

Green flags in a relationship could include basic manners like opening your door, very open with communication, respects your personal boundaries, reliable to you, daily words of affirmation, effort to know and grow with your family, shows empathy and feelings, and supporting your goals in life. In a healthy relationship, someone's green flags should definitely outweigh the red flags.

—Natasha

☁ **my thoughts**

Silverfish

*Your presence—I confided in
when I felt my world falling apart.*

Your hand I held when I was trapped in an endless cycle of codependency

*Funny, knowing that hand
kept me back
from all the happiness I could have had.*

*What I thought was support
was nothing more
than your way to ensure*

*I remained supportive while
you secretly held onto
the hope I was losing.*

*Then, you filled my head with false hope,
 and I trusted you
when you were only saving face.*

*Do you feel empty now? Do you
regret those lies you told?*

*Was feeding your ego worth losing me?
You had a troubled past and I was your friend, entangled in the trauma bond we
created*

*Never—will I ever again
let a "friend" so far in that my
eyes are blind to their flawed disguise.*

By Jasmine Saint Louis, *Brand Builder & ExCEL Fellow*

You&I

missing You comes in waves
and tonight i am
drowning,

what a dream
it would be
to come home to
You.

in the midst of
Everything
i still mourn
the loss of
You.

You're not
Gone,
my old friend,
but it's better...
this way.

because i loved
You
but i have
to love me more.
.

By Galiba Anjum, *Write to Lead Intern*

let go with love

Let's Connect: *When might a relationship with others cause you pain?*

Thoughts from the Cocoon Club:

"I was in a relationship with a person for 6 years, ever since middle school. We broke up when we got to college. This is normal for couples to break up before college, but I was super in love and thought this would be my forever relationship. We didn't see eye to eye. My partner wanted to see what else was out there before settling down while I was very set on my life partner. When we broke up, I was hurt, and it took a big hit to my high self-esteem. I wondered what I did and even questioned my worth for about 5 months after the sudden breakup." — Jasmine, ExCEL Fellow

"Due to my class scheduling, I have been with the same group of people for my whole four years [of high school] (I'm a senior now). Though we were a tight knit group, I've always felt lonely within the group. Almost like everyone had connections within the group (to other people) but me. Fast forward to my senior year, the group started to split apart due to personality differences. Looking at things falling apart, I started to realize these were never really my friends. No one tried to build an outside (of school) connection with me or even wanted to go out with me. My heart began to hurt because I was naive enough to think I had true friendships when in fact it wasn't anything like that." —Amber, ExCEL Fellow

Journal: *Are there any parts of hurtful relationships that you need to let go of to move forward (e.g., people, feelings of insecurity/rejection, anger, self-blame, etc.).?*

> "I had to let go of the memories... I had to be real with myself and the situation in order to let go. All relationships are not meant to last. If it goes then let it because God will replace it with something much better and worth the wait." —Jasmine

> "I had to let go of the fear of...not texting someone every day, being invited places, or even being known shouldn't matter to me. I still have to learn how to be by myself to truly move forward in my life." —Amber

Journal: *What would it look like to move forward from a place of love, rather than anger, hurt, or pain?*

"It was a very soul-crushing experience to move out of my hurt to a place of love. It's like giving birth in a way—moving through the pain to see the end result which is a new beginning/life (a baby)." —Jasmine

"It looks like me understanding that not every connection has to be a deep connection... and to be my own deep connection. This relationship taught me that true connections are very rare, and I can't force any connections on people who don't want that with me." —Amber

Lead the Way: What **affirmations** can you say daily to boost your confidence and show love to yourself and others (including people who have hurt you)? Circle your favorites or write your own.

- I am worthy of love.
- I am beautiful.
- I am special.
- No one can tear me down.
- I know my self-worth.

—Jasmine

- I am my own anchor.
- I am strong.
- I am beautiful.
- I am independent.
- I control my future.
- I can do this.
- I will not be broken.
- I am a fighter.
- I am courageous.
- I am enough.
- Letting go does not mean forgetting; it means moving forward.
- You do not need to seek approval of others to be valued.
- I love who I am becoming.
- I am allowed to feel.
- I am allowed to be angry and upset.
- My value or worth does not depend on the mind of others.
- I am meant for my destiny, not yours.
- I will move on.
- You are loved even when you don't know it.
- I forgive myself.

—Destiny, ExCEL Fellow

- Every experience (good or bad) is a lesson learned.
- I am not my mistakes or what I perceive to be mistakes.
- My presence is powerful.
- My hard work, tears, trials, and tribulations will all pan out.
- My imperfections are perfect.

—Amber

- I don't need to be perfect to be accepted.
- I am in control of my happiness.
- I will turn negative thoughts into positive ones.
- I give up the habit of criticizing myself.
- I release the past and live fully in the present moment.
- With every breath out, I release stress in my body.
- I am loved and more people care about me than I know.
- I give myself permission to heal.
- I accept the lesson my pain is offering me.
- I am ready to forgive anyone I feel has hurt me.

—Anthonette, ExCEL Fellow

our sheroes

By Joy Lindsay, *Founder & CEO of Butterfly Dreamz*

Compiling this year's **Leadership Journal** has been a true honor—a labor of pure love and absolute joy.

The Leadership Journal, Vol. 3: Let's Connect has proved to be a powerful and transformative tool for my growth as a leader, and I pray it is the same for you. I hope you treasure the thoughts you've written on your journal pages and that you've been inpsired and nourished by our girls' unique voices, beautiful art, and dynamic leadership.

I want to close out this year's journal by writing a special thank you to our **Butterfly Dreamz tribe**: our staff, our youth leaders, our Board of Directors, our volunteers, our donors, and all our family, friends, and supporters. Your love and commitment fuel us. Because of you, we have the courage and help needed to make our boldest "dreamz" our reality. Thank you! I love all of you.

"A woman is free if she lives by her own standards and creates her own destiny, if she prizes her individuality and puts no boundaries on her hopes for tomorrow." — *Mary McLeod Bethune*

The vision of Butterfly Dreamz is realized by courageous women—leaders who know what it means to put "no boundaries on her hopes for tomorrow." On the next few pages, I have highlighted some of these women. Their leadership is not just inspiring; it is necessary. They are breaking barriers, paving new paths, and making it possible for women and girls to *live boldly, dream big, and fly high.*

They are our **2022 Butterfly Dreamz Sheroes:**
- Danielle L. Scott, MSW, *New Jersey DCF Division on Women*
- Glenda Gracia-Rivera, *MPA, Rutgers Center for Women & Work*
- Sylvia Nelson Jordan, *Project sWish*
- Shameka Young, *Cognizant*

Thank you all for everything you do for our girls.

Much love & light,

Joy

Danielle L. Scott, MSW
New Jersey DCF Division on Women

New Jersey Rape Prevention and Education Director

DIVISION ON WOMEN

Danielle's Leadership Story

I have always known that I have been called to be the voice of the unheard. Throughout my life, I have been passionate about mobilizing communities and fighting against social injustice. I had no idea that this type of advocacy could be a career. I have been fortunate and blessed to have my passion and career align. I always say, I didn't choose social work, Social Work chose me.

Over twenty years ago, I began my career working for the State of New Jersey at the New Jersey Juvenile Justice Commission (JJC) as a Social Worker at the Valentine Residential Community Home working with incarcerated and delinquent girls. Desiring to affect systems change, I was promoted and became New Jersey's *first* statewide Gender Specific Services Coordinator. In this role, I monitored federal funding, developed and implemented delinquency prevention programs for girls, created and staffed a statewide advisory board (known as the Young Women's Action Alliance), established and hosted regional girls' conferences across the state (the Annual Celebration of Womanhood Conferences), provided technical assistance and conducted trainings on a local, state, and national level.

Currently, I am New Jersey's Rape Prevention and Education (RPE) Director at Department of Children and Families (NJDCF) Division on Women (DOW). In this capacity, I oversee *all* sexual violence prevention funding (state and federal sources) and the statewide implementation of programs and services. I represent NJDCF-DOW on a variety of commissions, boards and workgroups, as well as representing New Jersey nationally at primary prevention meetings, conferences, and trainings hosted by the Centers for Disease Control (CDC).

I believe that the uses of both qualitative and quantitative data are the only way to identify community needs and make informed decisions regarding programming and service delivery. Valuable data is gathered by speaking with community members and listening to their lived experiences, as well by reviewing statistics. My mantra and approach to her work has always been **"nothing about us without us!"**

I graduated from the University of Rhode Island with a BA in Communications Studies and Sociology the University of Pennsylvania an MSW from the School of Social Work. I am currently the Vice President of the Paulsboro School Board. I am a wife and a proud mother of 2 honors student athletes.

Glenda Gracia-Rivera, MPA
Rutgers Center for Women & Work

Director of Professional Development & Training

Glenda's Leadership Story

"Behind every successful woman is a tribe of other successful women who have her back."

My life has been a series of full circle moments... I literally grew up within the 4 walls of Planned Parenthood in the 70s and 80s, where my mom worked for 23 years of my life. Little did I know at the time that this would help lay the foundation for my personal and professional experiences in the long run. Empowering women and advancing gender equity has always felt like my key purpose in life, and I know now it's because I had an amazing group of women to lift me up from an early age.

This is why I work hard every day to pay it forward in any way I can. It's extremely important to me that we make it a priority to elevate women, particularly Black and Brown women, into places and spaces where we are seen, amplified, and affirmed. At the Center for Women and work, I get to work with women and girls from all walks of life, from the classroom to the boardroom, in a multitude of ways that helps me achieve this goal. Whether it's developing a program like ExCEL that focuses on sexual violence prevention, helping run a corporate mentoring program for undergraduate women at Rutgers, or guiding educators in how to implement a comprehensive strategy to improve their equity outcomes for minoritized groups, I am fortunate to have the opportunity to do such impactful work that aligns so well with my core values. I'm not sure how many can say the same, but my hope is that every woman/girl that I've touched in some way through this work, is also able to fully realize her own purpose in a way that is just as meaningful to her.

Sylvia Nelson Jordan
Project sWish Chicago

Advisor/Mother of Founder

I believe in myself and what I am capable of doing.
I am smart, clever, and willing to learn.
I am strong, steadfast, and can overcome adversity.
I am safe and loved by my friends, family and those that know me.
I trust my decisions and instincts.
I am important.

Sylvia Nelson Jordan says these affirmations to herself daily. However, they are more than self-encouragement. They represent the type of leader that she is: inspiring, caring, creative, and extraordinary.

Sylvia is a wife, mother, philanthropist, youth advocate and project manager. She has made a lasting impact on the Chicago community, particularly Chicago's youth, through her career at the Chicago Public Schools and supporting her son, McKinley's, leadership of **Project sWish Chicago**, a community-based organization that uses basketball to combat street violence and provide vital resources needed within underresourced communities.

Sylvia's love for Chicago's youth radiates in everything that she does, from planning memorable youth-centered events to creating meaningful work opportunities for young leaders. Sylvia cultivates safe spaces where young people can thrive, grow, and be celebrated for their unique gifts and talents.

Sylvia is a courageous visionary, and Butterfly Dreamz has been inspired by her dynamic leadership and her commiment to the Chicago community. Syliva believes in our community—and our ability to solve our toughest problems. She invests in local businesses, employs Chicago's youth, and advocates for community needs and change. Sylvia is a true shero.

To learn more about Sylvia's work with **Project sWish**, visit **projectswishchicago.com** and follow them on Instagram at @ProjectsWishChicago.

our sponsors

The production and distribution of **The Leadership Journal, Vol. 3: Let's Connect**, along with scholarships for our student authors, are made possible through the generosity of our sponsors.

utterfly Dreamz   cocoonclub.org/**join**

Made in United States
North Haven, CT
15 June 2022

20269648R10102